ROLISSA

══ Jane Lovelace ══

Walker and Company
New York

Also by Jane Lovelace

Eccentric Lady

Copyright © 1985 by Dixie Lee McKeone

All rights reserved. No part of this book may be
reproduced or transmitted in any form or by any
means, electric or mechanical, including photocopying,
recording, or by any information storage and retrieval
system, without permission in writing from the Publisher.

All the characters and events portrayed in this story are fictitious.

First published in the United States of America
in 1985 by the Walker Publishing Company, Inc.

Published simultaneously in Canada by John Wiley & Sons
Canada, Limited, Rexdale, Ontario.

Library of Congress Cataloging in Publication Data

Lovelace, Jane.
  Rolissa.
  I. Title.
PS3562.0857R6 1985   813'.54   84-15341
ISBN 0-8027-0800-5

Printed in the United States of America

10 9 8 7 6 5 4 3 2 1

=1=

ONE OF THE most impressive dwellings on Brooke Street was known far and wide to be the august residence of Lady Jennie Barnstowe. In addition to being eccentric, the lady had a forceful personality that affected everything she touched. Most often touched, and therefore a reflection of herself, was her home. An active, energetic person, she had a fondness for bright colours, particularly red.

Had it been one shade of red, or even more than one, used in moderation, the effect would not have been quite so startling. Unfortunately for those of delicate sensibilities, the head of this particular household was not one who believed in moderation. The entrance hall, stairway, and the main drawing room, all of magnificent proportions, were a shocking combination of pink and puce, with Turkey red carpets and magenta cushions. The varying hues waged a ferocious battle for supremacy from the bulwark of their heavy gold trims.

The only colours to break the rubicund riot were worn by the three occupants who sat close to the small fire, which brightened but failed to alleviate the chill of the early spring night. Normally, those females holding the social position of Lady Jennie would be out at one of the numerous routs and balls which filled the season, but at the moment, her niece and nearest relative, was casting the family plans completely asunder.

The hostess sat in the most comfortable chair, her shoes kicked off and her feet propped on a magenta cushioned stool, her viridescent yellowish dress quite casting the stool and the other furnishings in the shade. To add to the spectacle, she had removed the wig she wore to hide her sadly thinning hair, and those errant wisps that still clung to her scalp were protruding at odd angles. She sat tapping her fan on the arm of the chair and casting glances at her two guests.

The second person, a small, thin, and beaky little woman, dressed in a way and adopted an attitude that immediately put one in mind of a small wren that had been battered by the storms of life. She perched, for it was her way to crouch on the edge of a chair as if ready for flight, and let it be known she disapproved of something by the loud and suggestive sniffs she made behind a lace handkerchief.

The object of their joint gaze was the young woman, who appeared perfectly at ease. She sat on a footstool at their feet, playing with Mary Fitzherbert, Lady Jennie's cat. None could deny she was a picture worth painting. Her dark hair and beautiful complexion were set off by a small and finely shaped nose. If anything could be said to detract from the perfection of her other features, it would have been her mouth, for it was a bit large, but so nicely could it turn up on the outer edges that it was an asset in its very pleasantness. At this moment, however, a hint of obstinacy was forming Lady Rolissa Amberly's lips into a thin line.

Under the present circumstances, it was not to be thought wonderful that the young lady was feeling her sensibilities to be suffering some considerable strain. Until a year before, Rolissa could not remember a time she had not expected to marry Anson Talmadge, the current Earl of Ondridge's older brother. Some of her earliest recollections were of the brightly hued word pictures Flora Smathers had painted of the life Rolissa would live as the Countess of Ondridge. Anson's sudden death had robbed her of that future, but try as she might, deep grief for a person she had not seen since she was a child of four was hard to maintain. When the family began to plan to substitute Carson Talmadge in his dead brother's place, Rolissa listened, neither assenting nor demurring. While she had not truly accepted the idea, neither had she rejected it; the concept of a ready arranged life had been too strongly seated in her from childhood.

But now she was to have Carson Talmadge thrust upon her suddenly, at a public gathering, and to suffer the indignity of the staring, speculating eyes not only of the two families, but of numerous strangers. It was more than her carefully acquired aplomb could withstand.

Would she have felt the same if it was Anson she was to meet at Almack's the following evening instead of Carson Talmadge? Most probably, she decided, for she was convinced it would be no comfortable matter, meeting a betrothed, or any gentleman who had been held up as a possible, if not probable, husband.

Flora Smathers spoke suddenly. "They cannot marry." She nodded in short jerky motions, reinforcing the image of a small quick-moving bird. "If what I hear is true, I am quite shocked at you, Jennie, that you did not recognise it. Rolissa could never marry a man whose eyes were set that close together."

This remark, coming as it did out of a thoughtful if tense silence, had the effect of causing both Rolissa and Lady Jennie to start and gaze on Miss Smathers as if she had taken leave of her senses. Rolissa could not help but be shocked that her companion, who had worked so assiduously for the match, could suffer such an abrupt reversal of attitude.

"Flora, how can you talk so?" Rolissa was brought out of the doldrums by a consideration so unrelated from the purpose that it caused a laugh inadvertently to escape her lips.

Lady Jennie was blunt. "Flora, you're hen-witted, or you've been listening to rag-mouthed gossip. There is nothing at fault with the man's appearance. Indeed, his looks are quite striking."

Miss Smathers sniffed, making it obvious that she had suffered an insult through no cause that she could see. She raised her handkerchief to her face, looking over the scrap of lace with a doleful expression.

"Insult me as you please, Jennie. You were ever insensitive to the feelings of others, and why I should expect you to understand Rolissa's quite proper feelings of apprehension toward the man, I'm sure I don't know."

It was in Rolissa's mind to bear Flora off to her chamber, thereby putting a period to the contretemps, but she refrained. The energy with which Miss Smathers attacked Lady Jennie had taken years from the little woman's bearing. Lady Jennie's eye, sparkling with a martial light, also held a hint of pleasure. Rolissa had no wish to destroy their enjoyment.

"Gammon!" Lady Jennie ejaculated, her watery blue eyes bulging in her outrage. "Flora, have done with that missishness, and if you start into the vapours, I'll have you carted off. Stop badgering the girl about it."

"That's very well for you to say." Miss Smathers turned her head, so her suffering on Rolissa's behalf could be seen in profile. "You have not been accustomed to sacrificing for the child's happiness, and I am sure, while you might want to marry her off to the first available man to save yourself bother—"

"Oh, let's do speak of something else," Rolissa said with an impatient flick of her skirts. While they might take pleasure in their bickering, she was finding it decidedly vexing, particularly when she was the subject under discussion. "Really, Cousin Flora. Aunt Jennie would do no such thing, and I truly know you do not mean half the things you are saying tonight. I do appreciate your caring about me, but whom and when I marry must be my own decision, and I cannot allow anyone to make it for me." She rose, stepped over the numerous footstools and cushions dropped on the floor and crossed to the fireplace.

"I am for bed, and, Flora, I think you should be also. I am persuaded that when we accustom ourselves to the excitement and late hours of London, we will take small things less to heart."

She left the drawing room and was halfway up the stairs when she remembered she had left her reticule by the stool on which she had been sitting. She thought of sending a footman for it, but the young servant on duty had taken a seat and was dozing. Not willing to wake him, she returned and opened the door.

". . . and only a female as hen-witted as you, Flora, would believe Carson Talmadge would be capable of anything so dastardly."

"Hen-witted or not, I know what I heard—what honest gentleman would employ a cutthroat if he were not engaged in wrongdoing? And as for Anson falling from a horse, who would believe such a tale?"

"Rubbish! You did, just like the rest of us, until you let some viper-tongue fill your head with nonsense. I won't believe a word of it," Lady Jennie snapped. "Despite that abominable creature he keeps on as groom, Carson Talmadge would never have injured his brother. Come now, it's off to bed for both of us. Bringing out our girl is going to be exhausting . . ."

Rolissa closed the door and fled to the stairs, the reticule forgotten. So *that* was why Flora had so suddenly turned from being an ardent supporter of the marriage and begun degrading the Earl of Ondridge.

She was shaken by a chill that crept its way up her spine and lingered at the base of her neck. Flora believed Ondridge capable of murder—indeed of *being* a murderer! Then she shivered, throwing off both the idea and the feeling like a dog shedding water.

She could not accept what she had heard. Ondridge could not be the type to commit such a terrible deed. Dimly she remembered him when they were children. He was often rude and lumpish, but the affection that had existed between the brothers could not have turned to hate. She resolutely turned her mind to retiring, though her thoughts kept returning to the conversation she had overheard.

The next morning, Lady Jennie was alone in the breakfast room when Rolissa entered. In her morning gown of primrose India muslin, Rolissa felt very plain in comparison to the figure her aunt presented. Not fond of wigs unless she was going out, Lady Jennie had that morning donned a yellow turban with four orange ostrich feathers attached with a brooch. Her morning dress was a garish combination of yellow and red, and the sunlight that invaded the breakfast room fell on her skirt, jarring Rolissa's concentration.

When her aunt noticed her standing in the doorway, she waved her forward. "Come help yourself." She indicated the sideboard and the table in front of her where many of the dishes had been put nearer to hand. "That silly Flora is upstairs, moaning over tea and toast again— can't start a day on nothing, that's what makes her such a wet."

Rolissa, who needed no second invitation, turned from a dish of buttered eggs and shook an admonishing finger at her aunt.

"You really shouldn't tease her so. She may be a trifle high-strung, but no one could have been better to me through the years."

"All well and good, but up there in Northumberland there was no one to put a stop to those ninnyhammered ways. Mark me, we'll straighten out those fidgets of hers."

Rolissa said no more. All through the years in Northumberland, Flora had held Lady Jennie up to her as a pattern of sensibility and consideration for her indigent relative, a consideration that the rest of the world did not accord Miss Smathers, and which caused the good woman tremendous suffering. But when their visit was less than two days old, the poor downtrodden Flora had dragged numerous incidents from the time of their youth to prove to Lady Jennie that she was totally without the feelings with which she had previously credited her.

They ate in silence for a few minutes, and then Lady Jennie, who had started much earlier and had assuaged much of her large appetite, turned her mind back to Rolissa's problem.

'The prospect of meeting Ondridge look as black to you this morning as it did last night?" she asked with a knowing smile.

Rolissa sighed and pushed a bit of egg around on her plate with her fork. She kept her head down, not knowing how she wanted to answer and afraid her doubt would show in her eyes, no matter what she said. But complete honesty was best.

"Forgive me if I seem as much of a ninnyhammer as Flora, but how can I reach a decision so fast?"

"Foolishness, anyway," Lady Jennie snorted. "Beats me how anyone can expect to throw two young people together in a crowded room with everyone watching, and have them act sensible—" She paused while choosing another slice of sirloin, and then threw another look at Rolissa. "It's not as if we have to put an announcement in the columns this week, after all. Too much rushing—that's what's wrong. Can't see that it an do anything but put you both off."

Rolissa smiled at her aunt, relieved they were not going to be at loggerheads over Rolissa's hesitation. "I thought you were as anxious as the rest to see me married to Ondridge, and as soon as possible."

Lady Jennie's lips formed in a straight line for a moment, and it seemed to Rolissa as she watched that the dear woman had trouble bringing her expression back to one of casual concern.

"It comes to my mind that we should not have made too many plans."

Rolissa bit into a roll and chewed it thoughtfully, giving herself an excuse for not answering immediately. Her aunt's darkling look, coupled with yet another change of attitude in another family member, brought back that cold feeling of doubt about Ondridge. Obviously, Lady Jennie was less convinced of his innocence than she had indicated to Flora. But since she had not brought the subject out into the open, Rolissa, too, evaded what was of prime importance to both of them.

Lady Jennie set her cup back down in its saucer with a bang. "I still think it won't hurt if you look around first, meet more than one man." Now she arched her eyebrows playfully. "Every lady worth her salt has a court of admirers, you know."

She folded her napkin and pushed back her chair. "I think you'll probably be seeing a great deal of Ondridge. He can be a charming devil if he chooses. With your connexions and your father's fortune behind you, there will be plenty of young bucks around, but it will be your beauty that will draw Lord Ondridge, mark my words."

= 2 =

UNABLE TO RESIST enjoying the effect of his labours on his fellow servants, Jackson, the aging valet to Carson Talmadge, Earl of Ondridge, positioned himself on the landing and watched his employer descend the stairs. In the eyes of this gentleman's gentleman, the most critical of servants, the earl was worthy of the utmost in the care of his person. Seldom, even among the Corinthian set, of which the earl was not a part, was there to be found a figure of such elegance, yet with an athletic muscular development that would show the day's fashions to greatest advantage.

Not that Ondridge was complete perfection in the eyes of his valet. The earl's man might regret the military bearing with which his master held his wide shoulders. From that same army experience, the ex-captain might hold his head a trifle too high and lack a certain fashionable negligence, but there was no denying that his demeanour did not allow lesser beings any doubts that he was both a man of consequence and one used to command. No servant could be more pleased with the dark hair on that proud head, for it lent itself to the fashions of the day with an amiability not often discovered in its owner.

And if the appearance of my lord's face and hands were marred by being slightly too dark, occasioned by his being too much outdoors and not caring for his complexion, those same hands were quick, skillful and well-shaped, and that same face so aristocratically handsome that young women of fashion, and indeed all the maids on the premises, were said to sigh and dream of it at night.

But the earl, unaware of the admiration his person brought out in his servant, was descending the stair in a mood that would have sent the appreciative footmen scurrying for cover, had Carson Talmadge allowed his feelings to show upon his proud visage.

Not born to the honours he held, he was allowed as a youth the rough-and-ready activities he enjoyed, and his years with the army suited him particularly. He had been on the Peninsula when he received word of his brother's death and learned he had succeeded to the title, the estates, and, he thought wryly, all the disadvantages of elderly servants, particularly valets, who must be suffered in silence. He despised being fussed over.

He was at present almost at the mercy of his valet, due to an accident on one of his farms. A team of frightened horses had reared, broken their traces, and overturned a laden cart. Ondridge had managed to get himself in the path of some falling lumber. As a result, he was forced to remain in London for a few days, to allow the shoulder to begin healing, and to suffer the fastidious pamperings of his valet.

He entered the breakfast room and paused. Seated at the table, dressed for a morning visit, was his mother, Lady Carla. That she had left her room before noon was unusual, especially since her party the night before had lasted until the small hours. But for Lady Carla to be ready to leave the house any day at the unfashionable hour of ten was startling. Ondridge stepped forward and bowed over her hand.

"And to what do I owe the pleasure of your company at breakfast? A new shipment of silk! That's the only thing I can think of that would bring you down so early."

Lady Carla had partially turned to pour her son's tea, but she halted, the pot forgotten in her hand. Her dismay was apparent.

"Silk? Is there? Oh, heavens, and I have so much to do today. Dearest, if you knew of it, it was quite bad of you not to tell me earlier!"

A stranger would never have guessed Lady Carla to be the mother of a son just passing through his thirtieth year. Her trim figure was as willowy as in her youth, and the gold of her hair had lost none of its glow. She was a happy featherbrain whose only serious thought was for the comfort and welfare of her family. The earl thought her altogether darling and his eyes softened as he laughed at her distress.

"No, love, I don't know of a shipment of silk. I only mentioned it as a possibility. You must admit, it is unusual for me to have your company at breakfast."

Lady Carla, pacified, resumed pouring her son's tea. That she did so with extreme care was not missed by him. Slowly, she handed over the cup.

"This morning I have a visit to make—a very special visit." Her eyes fluttered up at him and dropped again. "I have waited so long, I cannot put it off until the proper hour—" Lady Carla hesitated, apparently in some confusion. Then she dropped her chin, seemingly overcome by a sudden shyness. "Lady Rolissa Amberly has arrived in London at last."

Ondridge paused, the cup halfway to his mouth. Willing himself to act naturally, he brought the cup up, took a sip, and carefully lowered it back into the saucer. He was aware it would appear odd if he refrained from making some comment. As he raised his eyes to his mother's, he saw she was observing him with trepidation.

"No doubt she will be glad to see you," he said with an attempt at casualness.

"No doubt," Lady Carla echoed, still searching her son's face.

With grim determination, as if his entire attention was centered on his appetite, he turned to his breakfast, though later, had anyone questioned him on what he had consumed, he could not have said. His mind was entirely taken up with his mother's news.

Rolissa. Rolissa had come to London.

Ondridge had not been long returned from the Peninsula after his brother's death when he caught veiled hints from his mother. Rolissa had been betrothed to his dead brother Anson since childhood, and he soon realised that both families, with their accustomed tenacity in seeking advantageous marriages for their offspring, were still hopeful of an alliance between the Amberlys and the Talmadges.

Since nothing had forced him to face the issue, he had put the matter out of his mind. After receiving word of his brother's death, he had sold out and returned to face his grief. He found the family affairs in a deplorable state. The protracted illness of his father, coupled with the gentle, easygoing nature of his brother, had allowed the estates to fall into serious disrepair. Mismanagement under inefficient and dishonest bailiffs was the major cause of the difficulty.

There had been no time to think of Rolissa.

Rolissa. What were her thoughts on this proposed marriage? Would she be as amiable to the plans of the two families as his mother seemed to think? Ondridge remembered her as a happy child, but one prone to be stubborn to the point of implacability when her will was crossed.

What were his own thoughts? he wondered. Was he prepared to accept the responsibilities of a wife? Did his current plans, so full of travelling, rents, repairs, bailiffs, and men of business, allow for the foolishness of courting? At the thought of attending *ton* parties, doing the pretty to a female while there were still such desperate needs among his tenants, his lips curled in distaste.

Still, sooner or later, he would have to marry. Anson, raised to the responsibility of the title, had understood that, and the realisation had been growing on Ondridge since he had succeeded to his brother's honours. He was assured that Rolissa had been well-trained to the position of countess in the expectation that she would one day fill it. He must provide an heir for the future, or the title would be removed to another branch of the family. He was unmoved by any motivation of his heart, but after all, if he found the chit to be passable—he dared not hope for a beauty—if she had countenance and would provide him a comfortable home and the necessary heirs, he should be satisfied. And there was his mother to consider. If she wholeheartedly approved of Rolissa, there would be no trouble having two women in the same household . . .

". . . I am not to say it, dearest? Of course, if you would rather I didn't, I doubt she will notice the omission." Lady Carla appeared disappointed.

"I beg your pardon?" Ondridge looked blankly at his mother. "I'm sorry, I was not attending."

"I asked if I might not deliver your greeting and say you hope Lady Rolissa had a pleasant journey."

Ondridge nodded. He considered his mother's suggestion to be an excellent choice. Courtesy without commitment would be the wisest course.

"By all means do so." He touched his wrenched shoulder, which had begun to ache slightly.

Lady Carla was instantly diverted. "Oh, dearest, you are so brave. Though you have said nothing about it, I have heard from the servants how you were injured in saving one of your men from serious harm."

"Aye, the captain is the bravest of them all, my lady," said Soames, the earl's tiger. He stood in the doorway of the breakfast room, obviously listening to the conversation.

Lady Carla stiffened. She was a person of gentle nature, and her care for her servants was well-known, but her easygoing disposition did not countenance poor training or familiarity in hirelings. More than once she had made it plain that she thought her son's sporting groom was odious in the extreme. She was suddenly frigid.

"Really. *Must* you allow this *pickpocket* in the breakfast room?"

"Humph," Soames, unabashed, grunted. "On the knuckle I was not! Her ladyship should know the high toby was my lay, and bang up to the knocker I was, too, until I ran up against the captain."

"I am not expected to understand him, am I?" Lady Carla said icily.

"No, Mother, but you *did* insult him." Ondridge could not resist a teasing smile. "You debase him by calling him a pickpocket, which to him is the lowest class of criminal there is. His misdeeds were of a more celebrated order. He was a highwayman. And by the by, he is here at my order. Soames, I dowant the phaeton this morning. Bring it round in a quarter of an hour."

"Aye, Capt—my lord, and I'll be on the watch this morning, should anything happen." Soames forgot himself and saluted as he left. His last remark boded such an air of impending catastrophe that Lady Carla forgot her disapproval of the tiger for the moment, so taken up was she with his last statement.

"What does he mean, he will be on the watch—are you in some kind of danger?"

Ondridge laughed. "Lord, no! *His* is the worthless neck I saved, if I did anything at all. Now I think he'd like for me to step into some difficulty so he can repay the dept."

"Darling, you have never before mentioned his background, but pickpocket or highwayman, there is hardly a difference, and others know about it. I have no wish to see you mistreat your people, but your indulgence of that one is causing talk. No one would say it to me, of course, but I did chance to overhear someone mention that it was strange that a man of such an obvious criminal nature could have a hold on you—" Lady Carla faltered and stopped as she saw her son's black expression.

"Well, they can damn well say it to me or close their mouths! My apologies, Mother, but Soames serves me, and served me well in the army, under fire."

"I'm sorry, dearest, I shouldn't pay them any mind. I'm such a featherhead. You must order things as you see fit. It's wrong of me to give you instructions as if you were still in leading strings."

She raised her head, smiling bravely as the tears hung unshed, which only served to make the earl more ashamed than if she had dissolved into vapours. He tried to make amends in the only way she might understand.

"All the blame is mine, Mother. If you can just abide my temper for a short time, most of the estate work will be settled. Then we can be easier. Tomorrow I'm off to—"

Lady Carla was dismayed. "No, not again," she cried out. "I had *so* hoped you would stay a little while in town and attend an engagement or two with me."

"I must make this trip tomorrow, love, but if it will please you, I'll accompany you to Almack's tonight."

"Would you, dear?" Lady Carla's face was at once wreathed in smiles. To get her handsome son out into society was more difficult than pulling hen's teeth. While she was trying to frame a more complicated expression of her pleasure, a footman appeared and bowed to Ondridge, informing him the phaeton was at the door.

In an effort to keep peace with his valet and his mother, the earl spent the morning adding to his wardrobe. Not only would he quiet the aging valet, but he would be prepared, should he find himself obliged, to do the pretty in society with Rolissa.

When the elderly Jackson learned that he was soon to be inundated with such a wealth of fashionable apparel, he was thrown into a state of ecstasy ill-becoming his dignity. He patted, smoothed, and fussed while the earl sat in stony silence, his teeth clenched to keep from heaping on Jackson all the lowest army cant at his most considerable disposal.

Even Lady Carla received a short greeting when he joined her, and while, on the short carriage ride to Almak's, he set himself to be pleasant, his demeanour as he greeted Mrs. Drummond-Burrell was still a bit grim.

The Talmadges had not been at the assembly above a quarter of an hour when the earl caught sight of his cousin, Lord Tulane, in deep conversation with the Honourable Mr. Jamison, his most frequent crony. But when my lord attempted to turn in their direction, he was held by the pressure of his mother's hand on his arm. With a start he realised why she was so insistent. They were crossing the room when a group parted and Ondridge was stunned by an outrageously bright shade of orange. Though the lady's back was to him, he knew the garish color in such a voluminous size could only be worn by the irrepressible Lady Jennie Barnstowe, Rolissa's aunt.

Ondridge stood by his mother, readying himself to meet Rolissa, for surely the young woman at Lady Barnstowe's side must be she.

"Oh, my dear Jennie," Lady Carla trilled as she and the earl approached. "I had no *idea* we would see you here tonight."

Never having been accomplished in untruths, Lady Carla's tone, so overdone, could not have made their duplicity more apparent.

Rolissa's back had been to them as they arrived, and as Ondridge made his leg to her aunt, he saw by the motion of her skirt that she was turning. He was glad for an opportunity to compose his face before rising to meet her.

The beautiful young woman who stood before him had fulfilled a promise not evident in the four-year-old child he remembered. The cream and pink complexion was the natural perfection that all blends of powder and rouge tried to achieve without avail. Her hair, a shade too dark to be described as brown, was nevertheless without the harshness of true black. Her height and slimness added to her poise and almost regal bearing.

But her changing expression gave him pause. As she turned she had been laughing, and the dark eyes sparkled with humour. Her greeting to his mother was of the friendliest. Then, too, she seemed perfectly amenable to meeting him—until the introduction was made, whereupon she seemed to freeze. Ondridge, lightly touching her fingers as he bowed over her hand, could feel an almost imperceptible drawing back.

Ondridge held in low esteem those gentlemen of his acquaintance who considered themselves irresistible to women. He would have been put off by any overeager response to his introduction, but the importance of this one, both in his eyes and in the view of the two ladies watching with such complacency, made Rolissa's behaviour all the more intolerable. In her eyes he seemed to read an assessment of himself, and a firm rejection. Intolerable, he thought, that she could gaze upon him for such a short time and dismiss him both as a person and as the Earl of Ondridge. Good God, didn't the girl understand her situation and his? The plans for the marriage between the families had been of such long standing that there was no graceful way out for either of them.

His more socially experienced friends could have handled the situation better, he knew, but most of Ondridge's adult life had been the rough-and-ready code of the miliary. Short of excusing himself from the company, which would be unthinkable, he had no idea what to do. Not only was his ego somewhat battered by this chit, but he was filled with a deep sense of injustice. If he had reacted to her in that insupportable way, he would be considered a boor of the meanest order.

Just then the musicians struck up a country dance, and the pointed looks, both from his mother and Lady Jennie, made it imperative that he entreat Rolissa to dance. Nothing was further from his desire. In fact, he heartily wished himself at Jackson's Gymnasium, where he could step into the ring and give vent to his frustration.

He was aware, as he made his invitation, that he had hesitated too long before doing so. His reluctance was abominably plain, but no more so than hers when she waited an inordinate length of time before offering her hand to be led onto the floor.

While they stood waiting for the sets to form, he assessed the situation and considered their stance; their silence was equivalent to that of two schoolroom children placed by the dancing master. She offered no conversation, but he was not going to be so backward. But what should he say to a young woman obviously so unwilling to bear his company? The experience left him feeling as if his head were packed with sheep's wool.

"I trust you had a pleasant journey to London," he said, as they waited for the set to form. He hardly recognised the haughty voice as his own. If there was a more banal way to begin a conversation, he was unacquainted with it.

"Quite nice, thank you," Rolissa answered, without turning her head to look at him.

The dance began and the steps took them apart. While he waited for them to come together again, he tried rehearsing charming remarks, but when he took her hand, his voice and his stance belonged to a wooden carving, and his opening remarks were such as one might have uttered if given the power of speech.

"I trust you are enjoying your stay?" The chit had no conversation at all.

"My visit has been quite pleasant, thank you." She offered nothing in return that would enliven the talk.

Ondridge's shoulder was now steadily aching. "I trust—" Did every sentence emerging from his mouth have to begin with those words? He knew it to be the result of his unease, his growing impatience with the girl, and he was angered by it.

"I trust—" Oh, Lord, he had done it again, but this time she interrupted him.

"Sir, I cannot think how you manage—you are the most *trusting* soul." Was that sarcasm in her voice? This, coming on top of his discomfort and the insult to his self-esteem, was more than his exacerbated temper could stand. He was well-aware he was making a cake of himself, and her pointing it out to him only brought out the desire to strike back.

"I beg your pardon," he said in freezing accents, "In a well-mannered society, it is the custom to make at least some pretense of enjoying your partner's company."

For the first time, she raised her gaze to his, and her eyes showed she had felt his hit. Her dark eyes had deepened with—what? Doubt, surprise, pain? He was not to be afforded a chance to decide, because nearly at once her expression changed to one of hauteur far surpassing his own.

"I beg *your* pardon," she said coolly, exhibiting more poise than he could at the moment feel. "But doubtless you are as aware of why we were thrust together as am I, and just as unwilling. I suggest we rub through this encounter as smoothly as possible and endeavour in future to keep a distance between us."

This rag-mannered rustic *was* rejecting him! His pride would no longer allow him to take her insults with complaisance. The dance caused them to separate; when they came together again, he expressed his sentiments in no uncertain terms.

"Eighteen years has changed you in looks and size, but that is all, I see."

Fire flashed in Rolissa's eyes, but since the dance had moved them to a position where they received the undivided attention of the hopeful families, her mouth curled in a smile. A smile, he thought with surprise, that was beautiful. The faint hope that they could laugh away the first discomfort quickly faded when she spoke.

"And I seem to remember a grubby boy who was, more often than not, rude and lumpish. I see he has added pomposity to his list of dubious virtues."

Ondridge, in that fleeting hope occasioned by her smile, had seen himself the stiff-rumped figure he was portraying, and would have admitted it, given a chance to do so, but her criticism had the effect of bringing up all his defensive guns.

"If I remember correctly, any rudeness on my part was occasioned by a willful little miss who insisted on trailing along where she should not have been—and, my dear, if I have presented an overly mannered impression, you might consider I am trying to make up for your lack!"

Good God, he thought. It was one thing to defend one's self, but that remark was unforgivable. He mutely watched her eyes as they turned again on him.

This time the previous doubt and indecision was entirely absent from her eyes as she turned them on him, and in their place was pain. He realized, all too late, that Rolissa's withdrawing, her cool poise, had been, like his, the fear of making a mistake in a time so important to them both. He suddenly wanted to take her by the arm and rush her out of that room so full of watching eyes to say, "Rolissa, we've made a mull of it. Let's introduce ourselves and begin again." When he opened his mouth, she had already begun her retort.

"You need not fear that I will be *trailing* you again. I can assure you I am no more desirous of your company than you are of mine. It is just as well that we met early in my visit—"

"Take care—" Ondridge interrupted, knowing she was about to make an irrevocable statement, and while he had driven her to it, he wanted, if at all possible, to undo the harm he had created. But she was far too upset to be stopped.

"No, sir, you wanted me to speak, and I will. Despite the desires of the family, your suit would not be acceptable to me. Consider yourself under no odious obligation, and I will do the same. Now, please take me back to my aunt."

The timing of her request had been perfect. At that moment the last strains of the dance ended, and there was nothing to be done but accede to her desire.

After a stiff bow, he left the ladies and went in search of his cronies. He would put her out of his mind. Obviously, he had ruined his chances with her. He would draw back and nurse his wounds, not the least of which would be the stabs of his conscience, since he had caused her as much pain as himself.

When he found the opportunity to pause and look back without being obvious about it, he took no solace from seeing two young bucks eagerly vying for an introduction. Ondridge wondered what perversity of fate caused such violent disagreement between himself and Rolissa, particularly when she was so beautiful.

But beautiful or not, she would make a damned uncomfortable wife. True, most of the argument had been his fault, but she had driven him to it, and that was not the way he intended to live his life.

Lady Jennie's prophecy about the earl's attention proved to be more optimistic than accurate. He neither left his card in Brooke Street nor attended any of the card parties and gala routs that were held that week.

Even if Rolissa's first visit to Almack's, which had also been her initial appearance in society, had been of short duration, it had served to make the latest *on dit* of the Polite World. The heiress, the niece of Lady Jennie Barnstowe, was a Looker of the First Stare.

Rolissa's days were entirely filled with poring over silks in the warehouses, visiting her dressmaker and the mantua makers, and shopping for slippers, shawls, reticules, fans, and gloves. Each time they returned home the number of visiting cards on the salver had increased. On the afternoon promenades their carriage rarely advanced more than a few paces before it was stopped for additional introductions.

Almost any young woman making her debut into the Polite World of London would have been gratified by the attention Rolissa was receiving, but for her it was a mixture of the enjoyable, the comical, and the exasperating, with the latter often overshadowing the others. Her first evening at Almack's had been such that would test the hardiest of spirits, and while she had considered herself one of the more durable, even she had been severely tried. That part of her irritation was caused by her own behaviour, which she considered boorish in the extreme, did nothing to alleviate her mood.

How, she wondered, could she have behaved in such a rag-mannered fashion to Carson Talmadge? Not when she had intended to be anything but pleasant when she met him, knowing the family was hoping for a match in that direction.

Meanwhile, invitations poured in and, as they were opened, it became a game between her and Lady Jennie to see if Rolissa could guess whether the hostess had a son, a brother, or a nephew who would benefit by a rich wife.

Miss Smathers chided Rolissa constantly for her cynicism, but Lady Jennie would laugh and point out that no girl of sense could take seriously the young fools who were making such cakes of themselves.

Added to the irritation of being odiously rushed by what she could only consider opportunists, if not actual fortune hunters, was the absence of Ondridge, the one man she did want to see. All her good intentions toward him had evaporated when he had been absent for two days. By the third she had decided to treat him as if she had never seen him before. She would let him know he was the most insignificant individual to enter her life. For two more days she stuck to her resolution, but she found it increasingly difficult to ignore someone who lacked the consideration to show up in order to be cut.

Lady Carla had visited several times, always bemoaning the fact that her son was still out of town. For the sake of her mother's dearest friend, Rolissa joined Miss Smathers and Lady Jennie in saying she missed him, and how unselfish he was to spend his time making sure his tenants' roofs didn't leak. Privately, Rolissa thought he could save himself the trouble by judicious choosing of his bailiffs, but that thought she kept to herself.

When Lady Jennie announced one afternoon that they should attend Almack's that night, Rolissa seriously considered pleading a headache, but hers was not a cowardly spirit. She accompanied her aunt there, to find an almost unbearable squeeze. To make matters worse, she was immediately accosted by Mr. Boscomb, not only the most persistent, but also the most boring of her recent suitors.

He was a stocky young man who affected to dandyism in his

clothing and a conservative attitude that caused Rolissa some amusement when she was not irritated by him. The combined situation of having pockets to let and an overbearing mother who sent him after every eligible female with a respectable fortune was said to keep him on the hop. Rolissa tried to be patient with him, as several remarks he had made led her to believe he would much rather putter around on his decrepit properties than do the pretty to a female, but she had nothing but contempt for the lack of fortitude that kept him doing as his mother felt he should.

Now he came rushing forward. "Oh—uh—I say, you are quite ravishing tonight," he stammered as he made his leg, holding her hand much too long and too tightly.

"Thank you, sir," she murmured, struggling to get free. She was at present wondering how she could escape his company, but his determined stance warned her his mother had told him to press his suit, and he was making a stalwart try.

"Uh—lud yes, ravishing," he prosed on, still gripping her fingers. "Eyes like stars—like stars."

Rolissa congratulated herself that she kept from showing her impatience as she worked her hand free. Eyes like stars, indeed! If there was such a thing as a dark brown star, she was sure no one would take the slightest notice of it, even if it could be seen at all. Then she chided herself for being so literal-minded. After all, Mr. Boscomb, his address most fustian and lacking in polish, was really only a very young man without the slightest idea of how to carry on a courtship. And even more tongue-tying was the knowledge that the sparkle fast developing in his eye had nothing to do with their different financial situations.

Just then Lady Sefton approached with two other gentlemen in train. Much against her strongest inclinations, Rolissa steeled herself to be charming, fervently wishing she had feigned that headache and stayed at home. As Lady Sefton confronted the younger woman, she opened her fan and whipped it back and forth, as if in some agitation. The look in her eye, however, was one of amusement, and immediately caught Rolissa's interest.

"My dear Lady Rolissa. I am quite undone by these gentlemen! They insist on an introduction, and threatened never again to attend our assemblies if thwarted in their ambition. Dire threats about rustication with broken hearts have assailed my ears. I do hope you know your duty to your hostess under such circumstances?" The famous Almack's hostess stood gazing primly at Rolissa, who threw her hands up to her face in mock dismay.

"Oh, Lady Sefton, what must I do? To be the cause of heartbreak is a thing most odious to me. *Far* more important, to lose you guests must be the solecism of the day. You must advise me."

Lady Sefton's lips twitched as Rolissa looked imploringly at her, and the hostess gave a haughty inclination of her head in approval.

"Your proper course, my dear, would be to let me introduce Viscount Tulane—a relative of yours, I believe."

The tall lord, dressed in a blue satin coat that set off his blue eyes and blond hair to advantage, bowed gracefully over Rolissa's hand.

"Merely a very distant connexion, child, and you need not regard it unless it gives me a claim on your time. For *my* part, you may disregard the low fellow who accompanies me. I do my best for the poor boy, of course, but you need not trouble to give him *your* attention."

The "poor boy" was obviously close in age to his companion, and no description could have been less apt for the tall, slender man with the hawk nose who was elegantly dressed in brown satin. He turned to Lady Sefton, his palms held up in a gesture of helplessness, a motion totally incongruent with the sharp-featured face.

"I beg of you, Lady Sefton, if my mentor has so cast me down, will you kindly come to my aid?"

Before Lady Sefton could answer, Lord Tulane intervened. "Dear lady, consider carefully. If he were to rusticate, it would be a mathematical rarity—the subtraction of one from society would become a plus for its members."

"Oh dear," Rolissa gasped, taking care to look perplexed. "Must one do sums for society as one does on the household accounts? And such a tangle when a plus should minus. Do advise me, Lady Sefton."

The jovial hostess was having difficulty containing her mirth, but by pursing her lips tightly she succeeded in keeping her smile at bay.

"Of course," she replied soothingly. "Let me take the responsibility of the decision from your shoulders by presenting to you Mr. Jamison of Wensley Place."

Mr. Jamison made a graceful leg and looked down at Rolissa

solemnly. "I pray, ma'am, that you will forgive me for being in my lord's black books. Alas, it was his nurse and not I that dropped him on his head as a child, but I was so thoughtless tonight as to remind him of the consequences." He pointed one pale finger at his temple and shook his head sadly.

"Most unaccommodating of the nurse, I'm sure," Rolissa replied with sparkling eyes.

"Oh, yes." Mr. Jamison nodded. "His parents thought so, too, I gather. Dismissed her without a character when she neglected to repeat her one talent." As he spoke, he removed his snuff box from his pocket, flipping the lid back with a deft motion of his thumb and offering it to Mr. Boscomb. That young gentleman had been standing the while with his lips parted in astonishment, but the offer from Mr. Jamison to try his sort was a compliment not to be ignored.

Mr. Boscomb had taken a pinch, but when Lord Tulane reached out a hand, Mr. Jamison took care not to see it and closed the box. At once Tulane began to fan the air with his scented handkerchief.

"Really, stripling, you try my patience." Lord Tulane was forced to tilt his head back in order to look down his high-bridged nose at his companion. "You *will* bring that concoction out in public."

"I'm so sorry," Mr. Jamison said meekly, and once again Rolissa was struck by the contrast between his sharp-featured countenance and his gentle tones.

"Well, don't do it again," my lord admonished. "Mr. Boscomb, I doubt he poisoned you, but if you should feel ill, please remove yourself from the presence of the ladies."

Mr. Boscomb looked shocked, but he was clearly affronted on behalf of Mr. Jamison. "But I assure you, sir, the mixture is of the finest. Quite unexceptionable—" He drew himself up noticeably, taking a deep breath as if physically enlarging himself to meet an enemy. "Dashed fine blend, I should say."

"Thank you, sir." Mr. Jamison bowed to him. "It is so kind of you to say so. I try, I really do, you know, but this fellow is forever giving me set-downs until I am quite undone." His look of patient suffering caused Rolissa to choke back a laugh.

She knew Mr. Boscomb was somewhat lacking in mental prowess and completely devoid of humour. He was not at all aware that he was in the company of close friends who delighted in nothing so much as trading insults. He threw a dark look at Lord Tulane, but he was all solicitude on Mr. Jamison's behalf.

"Really, sir," he commented, using his quizzing glass to inspect Mr. Jamison's attire. "There is nothing about your person to which anyone—" he flicked another look at Lord Tulane—"anyone knowledgeable on fashion could call you to task."

"Are you sure, sir?" Mr. Jamison looked up hopefully from his occupation of smoothing an imaginary wrinkle from his elegant coat and preened with some affectation. "My lord suggests this outfit is not at all the thing."

"Quite elegant," Mr. Boscomb gave his approval with all the authority of Brummell himself. "Much more so than many others I have seen tonight." He was not so foregone to courtesy that he actually let his glass rest on Lord Tulane as he affected to look about the room, but that it passed over the lord, there was not the slightest doubt.

To hear this callow youth giving the seal of approval to one of Mr. Jamison's address, especially at the expense of Lord Tulane, was fast throwing Rolissa into the whoops. She was hard-pressed to control her mirth when Lord Tulane came to the rescue.

"The music is beginning again. Do you waltz, Lady Rolissa?"

"Oh, yes, I—uh—I don't think—" Caught in a very awkward position, she tangled her words. She had no wish to offend him, but how did one say in front of an Almack's hostess that one had not been given permission to waltz at that exclusive assembly?

Lady Sefton came to her assistance. She closed her fan with a snap and gave the viscount a playful but admonishing tap on the arm.

"Really, Tully, you can be quite vexing. You deliberately put me in what could have been a most odious predicament. Thank heavens, it was in front of Lady Rolissa and not some of the others here tonight." Her frown left the gentleman not at all abashed, and her smile to Rolissa was genuine. "Dear, you must not miss an opportunity to take to the floor with this wretch. Despite his manners, his skill with the waltz makes him a treat for any lady he partners." She stepped back, graciously inclining her head, giving Rolissa the coveted approval.

As they swirled among the other couples on the floor, Lord Tulane smiled down at Rolissa, his blue eyes twinkling.

"This, I think, is a case of our saving each other. I kept you from unseemly mirth, and you saved my life, I wager."

"Your life, sir?" She was surprised at his statement.

"Quite possibly. The way Jamie is bamming Mr. Boscomb, the young fool just might call me out."

Rolissa gave him a smile more mischievous than mannerly. "Sir, I am persuaded that it might not be so dangerous. He would probably try for a head shot, and yours is particularly hard, if I understood the conversation?"

"Just so. Still, it would be my first duel, and to be called out over another gentleman would not be at all the thing."

"I see what you mean—perhaps I could help. To save your reputation, could you not say *I* was the cause? It would surely enhance my status as a heartbreaker."

"Ah, now there is a thought. If to the winner goes the hand of the fair maid, I will issue the challenge myself."

Rolissa frowned prettily and shook her head. "I confess to be flattered by the compliment, but what if Mr. Boscomb missed your head and did you some injury? I'd be required to marry him. I'm persuaded that I couldn't face spending the rest of my life being told my eyes are like stars or pools. Quite dreadful of me, I'm sure, but since my eyes are brown, I have an instant vision of mud holes. The thought entirely halts all romantic response."

"Terrible," Lord Tulane agreed, overdoing his revulsion. "I see you are a young woman with a very high degree of intelligence. Possibly you would prefer to be told your eyes are the brown of young acorns, that they hold the depth and softness of new cedar bark?"

"Why, how clever of you sir, to think of such things. I daresay I shall be quite overcome with such flattery."

"Then it must be my aim to carry it further. Let me see—the glisten of a just-curried chestnut, the softness of well-worn leather, the—"

Rolissa had been carefully taking note of his unorthodox compliments and could imagine several courses that they might take.

"All that is very well, sir, but I warn you, much farther into the stables, and you'll be dancing by yourself."

The lord's crack of laughter and his very awkward misstep drew the eyes of everyone in Almack's.

= 3 =

LADY ROLISSA WOULD have had to be more than human not to be a little gratified by the amount of attention she received. She was courted extravagantly, invited for rides in the park, and accompanied on promenades; parties to Richmond Park were made up exclusively so various young gentlemen could travel in her company.

If those beaux who were in need of a rich wife were the only ones who danced attendance on her, there would have been nothing to recommend itself in her popularity, but several of her ardent admirers were well-able to consider themselves in high pockets without recourse to marrying money. One of the highlights of her sojourn in London was the friendship she enjoyed with Lord Tulane and Mr. Jamison, who included her in their banter without offering themselves as suitors.

Several prune-lipped females had taken a perverse pleasure in imparting to Rolissa the information that both gentlemen were busily engaged in fixing the affections of other females. Lord Tulane's interest in Miss Singer had been well-known for some time, and Mr. Jamison had, since his salad days, been singularly faithful to Miss Marchlin, who lived retired with her family. Far from being discomfitted by the news, Rolissa accepted it with relief. While she enjoyed their company, neither prompted her heart to beat faster.

Though she was beginning to take pleasure in her social stir, Lady Rolissa was sometimes put to some effort to keep from laughing outright at the mannerisms affected by some of her admirers. Raised among simple people, she found fashionable attitudes among the young gentlemen somewhat ridiculous. Try as she might, she was unable to take them seriously.

One morning, when a steady fall of rain had kept her indoors, she found herself having to resolutely chase away recurring thoughts of Lord Ondridge. Both she and Lady Jennie were busy with their correspondence, and Miss Smathers was mending a flounce on her favorite and most hideous brown bombazine dress when the butler opened the door.

"The Earl of Amberly," he said quietly and stepped aside to admit a small portly gentleman whom Rolissa knew only from letters. Henry Fortesque, as the next male heir, had ascended to the titles of Rolissa's father on that good man's death. Now he walked into the room, his pale eyes peering nearsightedly.

"Well, hallo, Henry. Thought you'd be showing up soon." Lady Jennie greeted him as if he had visited only the day before.

"Between your cook and that excellent library, how could I stay away?" the earl said as he took her hands.

"Since you can't have either of them, I guess I'm stuck with you." Lady Jennie's smile belied her words. She brought him over to Rolissa. "I don't think you've ever met our girl face to face. Didn't tell her you were coming. Thought we'd make it a surprise."

Rolissa stood to greet her elderly cousin and was rewarded with a shy, almost absent smile.

"Dear me, child, you could have posed for the portrait of Lady Susan. With your beauty and charm, you could have been born a Fortesque—" He paused and looked round as the sounds of the heavy door knocker echoed through the house.

"Henry, you've had a hard journey in the rain," Lady Jennie said. "If I know you, you forgot to make your arrangements until the last minute and travelled all night on the stage. You need some rest. Come with me, else we will be inundated with young bucks and you'll never get away for a rest before tea."

Lady Jennie had just whisked Lord Amberly out of the room when Wiggins announced Lord Tulane and Mr. Jamison. Both gentlemen were dressed in the correct morning wear, with blue superfine coats, buff pantaloons, and shining Hessians. They had obviously arrived by carriage, since no drop of moisture had been allowed to mar their perfect outfits.

Jamie presented Rolissa with an invitation to an impromptu party being given that night by his mother. The occasion being the arrival in town of the young woman for whom Jamie had a decided *tendre*, he exhibited far less poise than usual. After staying for the prescribed fifteen minutes and trading a few insults, the two gentlemen took their leave.

At tea that afternoon, the subject among the three females was the entrance into the household of their scholarly relation.

Lady Jennie seemed pleased that he had arrived. "He's never a bother," she said. "Just shuts himself in the library and does his everlasting research and note-taking." She paused and looked over at Rolissa, waving a scone to ensure her attention. "Doing the family's history, you know."

"Yes, I do," Rolissa answered. "I'd like to know more—it sounds interesting."

"Good God, no." Lady Jennie shook her head energetically, "Don't encourage him or he will never stop talking about it. It's all that's in his head, you know. Sometimes I think they get a bit unbalanced on their subjects, these literary types."

"Oh, my dear!" Miss Smathers turned to Rolissa, rolling her eyes. "Henry's grandmother was a poetess, you know, and most certainly—" She paused, as if searching for the right word.

"Dicked in the nob." Lady Jennie's description lacked elegance, but served the purpose. "All those Fortesques get wound up in their subjects—"

"Why?" Rolissa asked.

"Who knows?" Lady Jennie, having finished the scones, reached for a tart. "One of his ancestors was disinherited, and since then most of them have taken off on high flights, to keep themselves busy within their limited incomes, I surmise. We may see a change in them now that they've come back into money, and with Henry having the title. Amberly provides a decent living, I take it?"

"Most definitely," Rolissa answered. "It would not support a wastrel, but my father's fortune was derived from it."

"Henry's pinchpenny ways won't be a drain on it." Lady Jennie laughed. "That coat he was wearing is ten years old if it's a day. Can't get that old fool out of his books long enough to see a tailor."

The conversation turned to the hastily planned party being held on Mount Street that evening by Lady Jamison. It was at this time that Lord Amberly entered the room.

"Ah, ever the family gathering," he muttered. "Just reading a diary of old Samuel Amberly." He shook his head sadly. "That lot had terrible rows over the teapot. It seems a shame that with their wealth and advantages they lacked the manners of my side of the family." After taking his cup from Miss Smathers, he walked over to sit by Rolissa. "But the young don't want to hear about history, there are too many exciting things happening in their lives. Young Ondridge escorting you, my dear?"

"He is not," Lady Jennie retorted. "He's not about right now, and even if he was, it would not do at all. Either Flora or myself will escort Rolissa."

Henry looked up, surprised. "Am I too old-fashioned or too dashing? I thought after they were betrothed—"

"But we are not," Rolissa spoke up quickly. She was afraid she was destroying his hopes, too, if he joined the rest of the family in their plans, but it was kinder to tell him the truth at once.

"There is no betrothal," Miss Smathers added with a shake of her head for emphasis. "The new Earl of Ondridge is not at all the kind of person—"

"Flora!" Rolissa's voice was raised in exasperation. "I beg you will cease this slander of the man's character. I declare, you put me to blush with your talk."

Her words had the effect of halting Miss Smathers for the moment, but Rolissa knew her elderly companion too well to expect that to be the end of the matter. Rolissa was glad to escape to her room after tea. While she hated to admit it, Miss Smathers had upset her with her suspicions of Carson Talmadge. As Lady Jennie had pointed out, good riders frequently fell. Rolissa's own father had done so, and, like Anson's, his last fall had been fatal. Still, there had been no suggestion of the tragedy having been anything more than an accident.

She contemptuously dismissed all the suspicions as idle but vicious gossip, but she wondered why it had upset her so. Was she giving more time to thinking about Carson Talmadge than she should? He was an arrogant beast, she told herself, so why did thoughts about him intrude on her concentration so often?

Because the rout at Jamison House had been given on short notice, it would not be awarded the accolade of being termed a crush, but it was uncommonly well-attended for an impromptu affair.

The party from Brooke Street was late arriving, caused by the breaking of a perfume bottle, the contents of which splattered and stained Lady Jennie's dress when she was fully attired. The eccentric female must then decide upon another outfit equally outrageous, and complete her toilet, so the clock was striking eleven when they arrived in Mount Street.

Rolissa had chosen to wear a soft apple green crepe, overlaid with pale yellow gauze, set off by an emerald green sash, slippers, and reticule. She was gratified by the approving looks that came her way, but her own attention was taken up with trying to locate her particular friends.

"Ah, there you are." Jamie approached from the left. "I had completely given up hope and felt myself slighted. You have no idea how easily I wound." His face was in its usual solemn mask and so stiff that often people were put out of countenance by him. Rolissa, try as she might, had not become accustomed to hearing soft words from such a stern mouth.

"Oh, sir, I am decided you could have done without me. Look at the lovely ladies that grace your home tonight—and I am led to believe I will at long last meet Miss Marchlin?"

Jamie's face was lit by a sudden glow, but what his answer might have been, Rolissa was not to learn. They were suddenly accosted by Lord Tulane, who had just led the lovely Miss Singer back to her aunt.

"You are too late in asking, child. Lady Rolissa is joining me for supper," Tully informed Jamie before he even spoke to Rolissa.

Jamie sighed and affected to dejection, but something about Tully's dress caught his attention and he raised his quizzing glass.

"I bow to your word, my mentor, but I wonder when she consented if she knew you would be bag-brained enough to wear stockings without clocks. I believe I will need a new bear leader." He leaned forward, making a show of quizzing Tully's stockings.

Far from being made uncomfortable by the attention to his apparel, the viscount shifted his weight, pointing his left toe and by doing so gave his companion a better view of his leg.

"Learn something, stripling. After due consideration, I have decided clocks don't add to a perfect leg, but perhaps they might hide the obvious defects of some I know of." Raising his own glass, he, too, bent forward, closely scrutinising his friend's carefully worked stockings.

Rolissa flipped open her Sevres fan and fluttered it with the appearance of extreme agitation. "One gentleman without clocks and the other with imperfect legs. I am of a mind that either of you would shame me dreadfully."

"Then allow *me* to lead you into the waltz that is forming while you decide," said a voice behind her.

Rolissa turned to face Lord Ondridge, who was dressed in wine satin trimmed with black velvet. He was at a glance the most elegant gentleman in the room, not because of his clothing, though no fault could be found with his attire, but because of a general air of poise and confidence that rested feather-light upon his broad shoulders. Before she could speak, Tully stepped forward.

"Gad, but it's been an age! If I hadn't known better, I would have thought you were rusticating."

"Just making sure I don't have to," Ondridge replied with a tight smile. "How did you do at Newmarket? Did that grey come through for you?"

"Worse luck!" Tully frowned at the memory. "Sprung a hock the first time out—the black did dashed well, though."

Ondridge raised his straight black brows. "Really? That's a setdown for my judgement. Wouldn't have thought she was up to the course."

Jamie laughed. "Then if you'd been there, you'd have been caught out with the rest of us. Tully came back high in the pockets at our expense."

"My felicitations," Ondridge replied. "If you can attend my small card party on Thursday next, I will endeavour to alleviate the strain of your bulging purse. You, too, Jamie. You owe me a rematch after the last time." With the same tight smile he turned to Rolissa. "I trust you will do me the honour?" He held out his arm, seeming to take her acceptance for granted.

Despite her resolution to make amends to Ondridge for her behaviour on the occasion of their last meeting, she was doubtful she would be able to bring those good intentions to fruition. As they took the floor together, she could feel her back and shoulders tightening under a load of tension. Would he see the discomfort in her face if she looked up at him? she wondered. But if she did not, would that not be a reenactment of their last disastrous meeting? He had seemed less haughty while talking with Tully and Jamie, but she would have been insensitive indeed not to see that he, too, was under a strain. Therefore his words, when he spoke, came as a complete surprise.

"Dare we break convention and reintroduce ourselves?"

Rolissa's gaze flew to his face. She recognised a certain wariness in his eyes but it was clear he was making a conscious effort to drive away the stiffness. True, his smile was only a caricature, but it was an effort at friendliness, she decided. He, too, wanted to begin again, to forget the unpleasantness. Her tension began to drain away and she dimpled up as she smiled.

"Why, sir, I do believe it would be quite daring. Will my reputation be quite ruined by speaking with a handsome stranger?"

"I hardly think so. If we speak oh-so-quietly, those around us need not know that this is an adventure some might find exceptionable."

Did she imagine it, Rolissa wondered, or did his step suddenly become much lighter, as if he had been released from some weight? Knowing he had been for much of his adult life in the army, she was surprised that he was so accomplished on the floor, but then thought it reasonable. The Duke of Wellington was said to enjoy gala occasions, and there had been many on the Continent, even during the war.

Around the room, eyes were turning in their direction as Ondridge swirled her through the dance. While some of the matrons might consider their steps a little wide and free for decorum, Rolissa did not care. No matter how she drifted in Ondridge's arms, she could not seem to keep pace with her heart.

She was just realising how she had been using her anger at him to cover the pain of what she thought to be his rejection of her. With the fading of those unrecognised feelings, she felt light and free in his arms, and when he looked down at her and smiled, his dark eyes were soft and fascinating. No trace of arrogance, stuffiness, or wariness remained.

"From the tales I had heard, I hardly expected to be honoured by your taking the floor with me," he murmured. "Everywhere I hear of the beauty of Lady Jennie's niece. Also of her wit and charm."

"Oh, yes, a most singular person, I believe." Rolissa nodded, not knowing how to answer a remark so blatantly flirtatious. "I hope to have the pleasure of meeting her sometime." Her smile was intended to chase away any doubts that she was teasing, and she was relieved that it succeeded.

Ondridge inclined his head, acknowledging her humour. "If a gentleman not yet known to be in the lists were to call in Brooke Street in the morning, should he be hopeful of finding a companion for a drive into the country?"

Rolissa appeared to think that over. "If that person had no prior commitments—and, to my knowledge, Brooke Street was expecting a very quiet day," she murmured. She had definite plans to accompany Flora Smathers on a shopping excursion, but under the circumstances, Lady Jennie could accompany her cousin. Rolissa was too enamoured of Talmadge's company to care a whit for shopping.

That part of their conversation being successfully concluded, the waltz was completed in silence, as if neither wished to risk another utterance that might break the spell of their new amiability. Ondridge led Rolissa back to Lady Jennie and made his leg to the colourful dowager, and with a last bow and a secret smile to Rolissa, took himself off.

Tully came strolling over and lounged against the wall, looking broadly disconsolate.

"I suppose I am not enjoying your company for supper," he said.

It was upon Rolissa's tongue to say no, he would not, but then, with a start, she realised that Ondridge had not asked to escort her in for refreshments. Somewhere in the recesses of her mind, she had expected, once their contretemps ended, that they would become inseparable companions.

She smiled sweetly upon Lord Tulane, thinking how generous he was to be concerned about her when he was well-known to be dangling after a lovely but shy young lady who was present that evening.

"What about Miss Singer? I am quite convinced you would rather be in her company."

Tully's normally placid expression turned wry. "Her dragon aunt has her own ideas of propriety, and according to her I have been awarded all the time I'm allowed for this evening."

Far from having her ego outraged by knowing she was second choice, Rolissa was struck by the humour of the situation. But far greater than the joke was the compliment Lord Tulane paid her. In the preceding days, she, Jamie, and Tully had developed a friendship of such honesty that the tall blond viscount could admit his true feelings, trusting her to understand his disappointment and need for solace. Her heart went out to him.

"After consideration, I deem it an honour to dine in the company of both a pair of perfectly turned legs and magnificent clocks."

Tully barked out a laugh that propriety had made him try in vain to hold back to a chuckle. "It isn't possible that even Jamie and I together have bested the Earl of Ondridge in the eyes of a female?"

No, Rolissa thought. Dear as Jamie and Tully might be, neither could ever reach that pinnacle of looks, charm, and manner upon which she had so suddenly placed the Earl of Ondridge. But she could hardly say that to her friend, who was still smarting from being turned away from his ladylove.

She raised her eyebrows. "I do not accept that it has never happened before. If it is indeed true, then I am of a mind that the ladies of London are very shortsighted."

With Tully, Jamie, and Miss Marchlin, Rolissa went in to supper. Their plates had been filled by the time she spied Ondridge. He was leaning forward slightly to hear his companion, a lady some years older than Rolissa. She was a small, slightly plump young woman with a look of quiet serenity. It was not her attitude but the earl's that arrested Rolissa's attention.

Rolissa had allowed Tully to lead her in to supper only because Ondridge had not asked her. She had tried to convince herself that he would have asked her, except that in all probability he was already engaged for that time before he had asked her to dance. That he regretted it as much as she, she had been positive—until she saw him giving the small plump woman all his attention. With a sinking heart, she knew by the intensity with which he listened to his companion that she herself was totally out of his mind at that moment.

Rolissa attempted to put all thoughts of him aside in turn, but found it singularly difficult. Miss Marchlin was a tall, bony female singularly lacking in beauty, but she was as quick-witted as Jamie and Tully. Rolissa was hard-pressed to keep up with the game of verbal thrust and parry. When the quartet of witty conversants returned to the main salon, they passed Ondridge, but he was so deeply involved in what his quiet companion was saying that Rolissa knew he was unaware of her exit.

She tried to shake off the deep sense of loss his inattention brought.

4

THE NEXT MORNING, when Rolissa, dressed in a pink morning gown, entered the breakfast room, the cessation of conversation at the table warned her she had been the topic under discussion. Lady Jennie, in a startling red brocade morning robe worn with an old-fashioned pink wig, was in the process of shooting dark looks at Miss Smathers.

In a particularly decrepit-looking brown dress, and fluttering her hands, Miss Smathers more than ever resembled a timid little bird. Even her nervous chatter reminded Rolissa of the din made by wrens in the fruit trees at Amberly.

"Did you sleep well, my dear? That noisy crier—I'm sure *I've* always *known* time passed at night without someone waking me up every hour, shouting about it . . ."

During Flora's nervous and disjointed chatter, Rolissa had taken her seat. She glanced at Lady Jennie, hoping to ascertain what difficulty had overset Miss Smathers, but her aunt was busying herself with a substantial breakfast. When it appeared that Miss Smathers might begin yet another line of complaints, Lady Jennie intervened.

"Flora, stop your blathering and let the child eat," she demanded, gesturing for Rolissa to turn her attention to the ham and rolls she had chosen from the buffet.

Lord Amberly looked up from the paper on which he was writing notes while he, too, put away a respectable meal, and frowned slightly.

"Rolissa, dear, are you sleeping well? You do look a bit fagged this morning. These little things happen and may mean nothing. Since you say you haven't any feeling for the man, does it really matter that he spent so much time with that woman?"

Rolissa dropped her hands in her lap and shook her head in wonder.

She smiled at her three relations, although she was seething inside with the irritation of having her every action seen, reported, and discussed. Even worse would be to have them feeling sorry for her.

"All this is a tempest in a teapot." She tried to laugh and fervently hoped she succeeded in what seemed to her a weak effort. "Do the three of you think Ondridge slighted me? Nothing could be farther from the truth. I was already promised to Lord Tulane." She threw a look at her aunt, who could have overheard her conversation with Tully, and thereby know she was dissembling, but Lady Jennie gave no sign of disbelief.

"Well, for my part, I would rather have heard you refused him because of your good judgement, rather than to have it have been caused by accidental circumstances," Miss Smathers retorted.

Lady Jennie glared at the little woman, but Lord Amberly stepped quickly into the breach. He gave Miss Smathers a wink as he gathered up his papers.

"Flora, have a care. It would not do for you to ruin your health in worry, nor give yourself a stroke. Since Rolissa shows no evidence of rushing into marriage, she may need you for quite a while to come. You put me in mind of Jane Deversly back—oh, must be 1438 or thereabouts." He shook his papers for emphasis. "Drove herself into heart failure trying to protect her ward, and as a result the girl was left without an adviser. Everything poor Jane was trying to prevent came true—probably because she wasn't there to prevent it."

Rolissa gave a small sigh, wishing there was some way she could explain to Henry that while he thought he was helping, he was only building a false self-esteem in Flora that could later be quite vexing to everyone.

"Well, I do worry about her." Miss Smathers had been much struck by having her heroic efforts on Rolissa's part recognised. To more fully fit the part of one whose worthiness went unsung, she took out her handkerchief and gave a self-pitying sniff.

"And well you should, but remember, for an Amberly, she is certainly no muttonhead. Her good judgement and yours will prevail—yours, too, Jennie."

Lady Jennie put her napkin aside and rose from her chair. "Henry, I see now, we'll have to keep you here. One thing I can say for you, you're a peacemaker." She turned a look of dissatisfaction on the table.

"I want more tea, and I want it in the drawing room. This chair is dashed uncomfortable. I don't know why I allowed myself to be talked into buying it. Come along, everyone. Flora, stop playing with that roll—you're not eating it."

When the family had followed Lady Jennie into the red drawing room, the hostess ensconced herself in a thronelike chair by the fire and turned to the subject of the woman Carson Talmadge had led in to supper the night before.

"This whole upset amounts to nothing," Lady Jennie said complacently. "Everyone thinks Ondridge has a new amour, and it's no such thing. The female was Lady Handing, the widow of one of his army friends. Only natural he should pay her some attention. Probably have a lot of memories in common. She's been widowed for two years, and she's in London to bring out her sister. The girls are the orphans of old Viscount Winsley."

"I am persuaded he is the one who married a wealthy cit's daughter," Miss Smathers intervened, her face alight with gossip.

"The same." Lady Jennie nodded. "With him dying and not having any female relatives, it's up to Lady Handing to bring out her sister. Myra Sefton says there's some trouble between the girls and their commoner connections. The cits would like to keep both of them unmarried. Don't want them making matches in the *ton*. Seems they want to keep control of the girls' purses."

"Shocking," Miss Smathers cried, and then brought herself up short. "Still, perhaps it might be better for Lady Handing and her sister to listen to their elders, rather than involve themselves with the wrong sort, even if they are well-born." Here she cast a sly look at Rolissa, but, used to Miss Smathers's warnings, that young woman let the remark go unheeded.

Just then the door opened and Wiggins entered to announce Lady Carla and the Earl of Ondridge.

Lady Carla came tripping into the room, her excitement evident and her face aglow. She rushed straight to Lady Jennie.

"*Dearest* Jennie, do forgive me for disturbing you so early, but my dear son has so generously offered to take me to Luthforth to see Cousin Sadie, and I want to steal Rolissa away. Sadie is a relative of hers also, and what a pity that they've never met! I am quite certain they will be enchanted with each other. Oh, do say I may have her for the day!"

Rolissa stared in astonishment at this unexpected turn of events. Lady Carla was so pleased, so excited, it seemed she could make the trip to Luthforth and back without a carriage and hardly touching her dainty feet to the ground.

Rolissa's gaze sought out Ondridge, who had just turned from greeting Lord Amberly and whose own attention rested on his animated mother with approval. At first Rolissa had been slightly dismayed, since she had been looking forward to the ride that she assumed would only include themselves and possibly a silent groom on the back of the phaeton, but she could see that this excursion would have the affect of prolonging their time together. And who could be a more willing chaperone than Lady Carla, Rolissa thought with affection.

As her glance moved away from Ondridge it chanced to fall on Miss Smathers, and for a moment she felt a thrill of dread. So set and disapproving was her companion's face that any moment she expected to hear the dear women's fears come tumbling out, to the severe embarrassment of everyone present. In the interest of preventing a total annihilation of the friendship between the two families, she spoke up.

"Dear Lady Carla, I can think of nothing I would rather do, though I fear I will delay you while I must dress for the journey."

Lady Jennie, always forthright, was quick to settle the situation.

"So get along with you and change your clothes, else you will be well after dark getting back." She waved Rolissa out of the room and with the same motion gestured for Ondridge to sit beside her. "Now tell me something, young man—I've been hearing about those improvements you're having made at Wellesley, and my bailiff thinks— Flora, don't go, I want you to show Carla . . ."

The strident voice of Lady Jennie faded as Rolissa closed the door to the drawing room. Her steps were feather-light as she crossed the hall, hurrying in hopes of finding Maggie still puttering about in her room. She had no wish to delay the start of the journey by even a moment.

As Rolissa was dressing, Flora slipped into the room. Her face was set in a disapproval she saw no need to hide.

"If I may have a few moments, I will dress and go with you," she said firmly.

Knowing the dear woman's concern, Rolissa tried hard to be patient. "Dearest Flora, you may not. It will only add to the awkwardness. I am convinced, feeling as you do, you could never be in Lord Ondridge's company for more than a few minutes without causing all of us to suffer mortification. I know you have some reason for disliking him, but no matter what your fears, I will be in the company of his mother."

But Flora was not to be so easily dissuaded. "You don't know the dreadful tales I have heard about that man," she said, lowering her brows and speaking in ominous tones.

It was Rolissa's intention to wave away Flora's worries and pay them no mind, but she knew as long as the dear little lady was in the room, there would be no stopping her. In addition, Maggie was listening with open mouth. The last thing Rolissa wanted was to have more loose talk among the servants. She sent Maggie to look for a pair of stockings in the drying room, and then turned on her companion.

"Now, Flora," Rolissa said, frowning at Miss Smathers. "You have yet to tell me exactly what you have heard that has so put you off Carson Talmadge. If you wish that I shall take your advice to heart, you must give me the reason behind it."

Faced with the necessity of speaking plainly, Miss Smathers wrung her hands and turned away, staring at the brushes laid out on the dressing table.

"After meeting him, I am persuaded he is not the man for you," she said finally.

"Flora, that is not at all the truth," Rolissa answered. "I am well aware you have heard some gossip that causes you to think he had a hand in his brother's death, and I am quite sure nothing could be farther from the facts in the matter. He was on the Continent with the army when Anson fell from his horse."

"But that dreadful tiger of his was in England, and everyone says the man obviously has some hold over the earl to behave as he does."

Rolissa, exasperated, shook her head. She might come to dagger-drawing with Ondridge, but she could not believe he would have desired Anson's death.

"And another thing," Miss Smathers continued breathlessly, after seeing she had not made the desired impression on Rolissa. "Have you never thought how much wealth would be his if this marriage takes place? Rolissa, dearest, let me go with you, let me protect you."

"Flora, these suspicions are foolish and without any foundation. Anson was known as a neck-or-nothing rider, and there is no true suspicion that his death was anything but an accident. You cannot condemn a man because of his strange taste in servants, you know."

At that moment Maggie came bustling into the room, full of new importance. She scolded and insisted she had known from the first that the stockings she had been sent to find were a bad choice, and Rolissa let her give full voice to her opinions in order to keep Miss Smathers from issuing any more warnings.

Maggie rushed Rolissa through the rest of her toilet and followed her down the stairs, carrying her sunshade, her gloves, and her reticule. Rolissa had hardly caught her breath before she was in the landau and rolling north toward Bedford with the Earl of Ondridge and the dowager countess.

Knowing that most gentlemen of athletic prowess preferred riding to suffering the stuffiness of enclosed vehicles, Rolissa was surprised that Ondridge joined her and Lady Carla in the landau, taking the forward seat. They were hardly out of sight of Barnstowe House before it became evident that he had set himself to be a charming and gracious companion.

Rolissa was determined that nothing should spoil the day, and deliberately put aside all thoughts of Flora's warnings.

Ondridge interspersed his conversation with comments about the lands on either side of the road. He mentioned the improvements he noticed, and his thoughts on what would give the landholder a better output. Since her father had always taken an intense interest in his properties, Rolissa was able, if not to add some brilliant advice, at least to make suitable comments that showed her understanding.

When Lady Carla showed signs of being bored with the conversation, Talmadge would change the subject, giving no indication that he was impatient with this parent who would rather discuss a hand of whist than the lands that were the source of her funds.

As Lady Carla had promised, the drive was pleasant, the day was warm, but not uncomfortably so, and the rolling fields added a very pretty picture.

Luthforth, too, was all that Lady Carla had said it would be. When they arrived, no welcome could have been warmer than the one they received from Lady Carroge. Their hostess was a meek little woman who affected mourning clothes, though Lady Carla had confided to Rolissa on the way that the viscount had been dead for more than twenty years. Since their hostess hardly looked to be in her fortieth year, Rolissa was persuaded she must have been widowed very early in her marriage.

The lovely old house, not displaying any particular style, since it had been added to throughout the years, was a mellow, comfortable abode. The furnishings were a hodgepodge of varying periods and contained some very impressive lacquered pieces brought back from travels in the Orient.

Luncheon was all that anyone could have asked. The soup was removed with a loin of veal and pigeons *à la crapaudine,* and a *capilotade* of ducklings served with asparagus, jellies, a dish of *peu d'amour,* and gooseberry pie completed the meal.

On any other occasion, Rolissa would have enjoyed herself immensely, but the looks that Lady Carla kept giving Rolissa and Ondridge as they sat across from each other were enough to make any female of the least sensibility dissolve into tears of embarrassment. In spite of the discomfort, Rolissa could not but love Lady Carla. Clearly, the woman lacked both the intelligence and the tact to handle the situation gracefully, but her determination for what she considered the best course for both parties had to be admired.

Rolissa was relieved, when they rose from the luncheon table, to be invited by Ondridge to ride out with him, but Lady Carla's lively astonishment and excess of delight at the suggestion further discomfitted Rolissa.

Ondridge handed Rolissa into the tilbury that had been brought to the door. Since it was a two-seated vehicle, leaving no place for a groom, she would be alone with him. As though he could read her mind, he gave a crooked smile that for once seemed genuine and held great tenderness.

"As boring as estate business may be, I think you will find it more comfortable than spending the time listening to the hints of my mother." Completely at ease, he leaned against the backrest and gave the farm horse the office to start. He seemed as much at home with the slow, plodding animal as he had on the dance floor at the Jamison rout. But his every move reinforced the aura of capability, and driving an old cart horse took away not one whit from the elegance of his person.

As they left the carriage drive and turned onto a track that served the barns, he slowed the horse and inspected an outbuilding with an intensity that caused Rolissa to turn, attempting to see what required such concentration. To her the structure seemed unexceptionable, and the only thing of note was the light, unweathered wood of a number of new shingles and several boards on the side of the building. Throughout the complex of farm structures, she saw the evidence of recent repairs, and it was growing more apparent by the moment that Ondridge was on a tour of inspection. Twice he pulled a small notebook from his pocket and made quick jottings, but as they left the barns behind and struck off down a track between two fields, he nodded thoughtfully and seemed satisfied.

"Is Luthforth one of your properties?" she asked in surprise.

He nodded. "It's taken some work to bring it back to a decent condition," he remarked, and halted the tilbury, pointing across a field. Several workers were industriously labouring in a drainage channel. "There's still a lot to be done before it's paying its own way again."

Rolissa said nothing, and he drove on, looking to the right and the left with every evidence of pleasure. To her eye, nothing seemed amiss, but neither was there a cause for joy. The field on the right was tinged a light green by a crop that had reached the height of no more than a handspan, and to the left the ground was newly furrowed. Here and there she thought she saw small green wisps in rows, but they were too small and as yet too uneven in their growth for her to be sure she was looking at another planting.

Farther on they came upon a group of small, thatched cottages. Several, like the cluster of the home farm, showed evidence of recent repairs, but one caught her eye. The state of dilapidation was appalling; the walls and roof sagged, and no repairs had been attempted. In front of the door, several children were playing with a litter of puppies.

"If you've been so conscientious about the rest, I wonder why you've made no repairs there," Rolissa observed.

"Repairs on that one would be futile." A darkling look came into his eye as he looked back at the sagging cottage. With a gesture that spoke both disgust and impatience, he whipped up the horse and drew up at a house under construction. By the road, leaning against a fence post, was a boy of approximately ten years, a ragged little urchin in a torn cap. He looked up as the tilbury came to a halt, tugged his forelock in greeting, and turned back to watch the construction, neither speaking nor shifting his position.

Ondridge took the boy's offhand greeting in his stride. "Will it do, Tom?" he enquired with a trace of a smile.

"Hmm—I think so. Ma likes it—it's a mite bigger'n what we got now." Tom straightened and strolled over to the tilbury, pulling his forelock again to Rolissa, but his gaze turned to Lord Ondridge. "You goin'ta buy that bay of Mr. Wainsbrook's? Saw him jumping t'other day. He don't look as good in the field as he does in the stable. Jumps off his hocks."

My lord raised his brows and looked thoughtful. "You suggest taking another look at him?"

"Think mayhap you better." With another nod, Tom strolled off in the direction of the half-ruined cottage, no more awed by the earl than were the gamboling puppies they had passed.

"One of my chief advisers," Ondridge explained as he flipped the reins and gave the farm horse the office to start.

"Will you take another look at the horse?" Rolissa asked, looking back over her shoulder as the child strolled on down the road.

"I wouldn't wager against it," Talmadge replied, his face serious. "The boy has a natural talent for judging horseflesh."

For more than an hour they wound about the rutted tracks. Once he halted, and, stepping down from the buggy, he tested the strength of a newly mended fence. Satisfied, he took his seat and started off again. At times, he seemed to forget Rolissa was beside him, but more often he spoke volubly about his plans for Luthforth. She knew he was caught up in his subject, but the warmth with which he confided his ideas showed her an unexpected side of his character. She realised she was truly at ease with him for the first time, and that ease made her tongue unwary.

"You really *enjoy* this," she observed. "I had wondered why you didn't leave it to your bailiffs, but you like being out here." She was at the moment thinking not so much of him as of her father. Though he had no talent for farming, and his ideas were often impractical, he was forever in his bailiff's way, either advising or asking questions.

Lord Ondridge, it seemed, read an entirely different meaning into the observation she had made. His brows lowered.

"Why shouldn't I like it? These are my land and my people. Who'd have more interest in seeing it and them properly cared for?"

Rolissa was stung by his outburst, and considered herself unjustly censured, when her remark had been occasioned by the most innocent of feelings. She truly meant to hold her tongue, but her earlier resentment was still close to the surface of her emotions. She gave him a look of queenly hauteur.

"Then it seems to me that you would have taken better care of it in the past. If you've always been of such a mind, how did that cottage fall into such a deplorable condition?"

"Luthforth is part of the entailment," Ondridge snapped. "Until it came into *my* hands—" He stopped speaking abruptly, his lips tightening.

Rolissa bit back a retort. Unthinkingly, she had somehow given him the impression she thought him in the wrong, and just as impetuously, she had struck back when he defended himself. But why had he felt the need? she wondered. Still, after his efforts the night before to put a stop to their disagreement, she could not but feel she owed him the same effort.

"My goodness," she said with false brightness, "I do tend to give you the wrong impression of what I'm thinking."

"I thought you were plain enough," Ondridge replied stiffly.

"About the cottage?" Rolissa waved away the idea with one gloved hand, wishing he would not make it difficult for her to smooth over the incident. She looked up candidly. "A mistaken feeling that I must attack to defend myself, when all I meant by the first remark was that my father also enjoyed inspecting his properties and seeing that everything was in order—"

"Forgive me," Talmadge interrupted, his smile indicating that his good humour was once more restored. "I should be thrown from the carriage and trampled beneath the feet of old Dobbin. I seem to be a bit touchy on some subjects, and I do apologise."

"*I'll* forgive you." Rolissa laughed. "But I doubt Dobbin will if you put him to such effort. I am persuaded he has neither the strength nor the disposition for trampling."

"Oh, but I have it on the authority from Tom that he was quite a fellow in his day," Ondridge replied. "Colt and horse, he's been at Luthforth long enough to be considered a family retainer."

Vaguely, in their often interrupted drive, Rolissa had been aware of the earl's patience with the old horse, but now she realised that not all of Ondridge's stops had been by his design. As if to point that out, Dobbin came to a halt, leisurely grazed on the grass growing in the middle of the cart track, and then moved on again. In view of Ondridge's reputation as a whip, Rolissa could only admire the sensitivity of feeling that made him allow the old animal to set its own pace.

Surely a man who cared for young boys like Tom and animals like the ancient Dobbin would never harm his own brother, she thought. But a perverse little logic raised a unbidden challenge. Would he not value even old horses and children on a property for the gain of which he would kill his brother?

Rolissa pushed the thought aside, forcing her mind to absorb the vista of a wooded copse in the distance, the long rows of a cultivated field where light green shoots were just visible above ground. On the other side of the track, a lush pasture was dotted here and there with buttercups.

Beside her, Lord Ondridge, with no idea of her conflicting thoughts, seemed complacent. Several times his eye turned to her, and the admiration she read there filled her with a *frisson* of delight. Lady Jennie had told her Talmadge would not be drawn to her by her fortune, and to Rolissa it seemed her aunt was right. Ondridge's gaze seemed to hold a quality of appreciation that was for her alone.

But as they rode in silence, the frequency of their looks at one another and the intensity in his eyes began to embarrass her. She was aware of the impropriety of their ride, alone and unchaperoned. As if he too felt the breach of convention, he whipped up old Dobbin and shortly turned through a gate that opened onto the public road.

The old horse, recognising the direction that would take him back to his stall, moved along at a good clip for some minutes. Then, tiring, he slowed. Again, Ondridge allowed the animal to set its own pace.

"Marchlin Hall." He indicated an imposing structure set in a grove of ancient oaks. "You met Elsa at Lady Jamison's."

"A lovely young lady," Rolissa said, trying to prove she could be gracious and complimentary, though the last thing to be said about the young female in question was that in looks she was anything less than an antidote.

"Lovely?" Talmadge gave a bark of laughter. "Beak-nosed and butter-toothed is more like it. But give Elsa Marchlin her due, she's a right one, and a bruising rider."

Rolissa matched his mood. "It's a shame that so many admirable talents do not display well in the drawing room."

There was little in their remarks to bring such a glance of tender accord from him, but as Rolissa was bathed in his look of approval, she smiled back. She was very glad that she had accepted his invitation, and fervently hoped there would be many more.

=5=

ROLISSA AND THE Talmadges remained at Luthforth Manor only long enough to partake of some refreshments before starting their journey back to London. Before they were long on the road, Lady Carla began to doze, and the young members of the party forebore conversation in consideration of her slumber.

Rolissa was pleasantly tired, but her mind was too full to sleep. She was thinking about the earl, who had shown her a multiple of faces that day. Which one was truly the new Earl of Ondridge? Was it the man with the ruthless voice, who was determined to have life his way, or the sympathetic, considerate person who talked with the farm lad as if he were an equal?

His treatment of the boy stayed uppermost in her thoughts, no matter that she tried to remind herself of other less attractive parts of Ondridge's character. No man, she thought, who was kind to children and animals could be a villain. The idea that he could have been showing a false side for her benefit intruded for a moment, but was quickly banished. The child had approached the tilbury with the calm assurance that he would be heard, showing without a doubt that his dealings with his lord were of some previous standing.

Why, she wondered, did it matter so much? But Rolissa, being a person who was as straightforward with herself as with others, knew the answer. Despite all her earlier feelings, she was being drawn to the man, while, in part, the suspicions of him that were circulating within London society certainly made him unacceptable until the truth of the issue was known. And within herself, she could feel impatient of that only obstacle to what she was beginning to see as her happiness.

During the next days, she was to have ample opportunity to see the earl at unguarded moments. Apparently, there had developed a lull in the necessity for him to be constantly on the road between his properties, and he appeared content to reside in Berkeley Square. Far from adopting the stiff, haughty attitude he had evidenced during their earlier acquaintance, he seemed to be all in accord with his mother's wishes that he further his friendship with Rolissa. Nor, in the occasional glance when handing her into a carriage, taking her hand on the floor, or in the few minutes of private conversation allowed them, did the romantic endeavour appear to be only on the part of his doting parent.

The time they spent together was, in truth, made uncomfortable by Miss Smathers. Her doubts, as far as Rolissa could determine, were not greatly reinforced by the entire *ton,* who, growing more used to the earl's tiger, had taken to more current gossip. But once Miss Smathers had conceived an idea, a team of oxen could not separate her from it, and with the added incentive of protecting Rolissa, she was indeed tenacious. She laid aside her dislike of going out in society in order to protect her charge, but dire warnings from both Rolissa and Lady Jennie, as well as Miss Smathers's own affection for Lady Carla, kept her tongue still.

On the first night that the residents of Berkeley Square and Brooke Street entered society as a party, Rolissa had been acutely uncomfortable, caught between the effervescent Lady Carla and the disapproval of Miss Smathers. What was more, they had no sooner arrived at the opera house than she discovered that seeing the infamous earl and young Lady Rolissa Amberly together seemed to be of more interest to the London *ton* than the scheduled performance. Nor was she comfortable at the first routs and the ball they attended; Ondridge's every attention to her—and she had to admit they were many—was openly watched and discussed by all but those who were busy about their own courtships.

As the pair was more and more in each other's company, both the frequency and the tone of the earl's efforts for her comfort and entertainment were becoming more marked. Rolissa found herself dreaming of him at night, and growing less patient with Miss Smathers's suspicions. Her irritation grew also with Lord Amberly, who, wanting peace at the table, was puffing Flora up in her own conceit in his efforts to soothe the drab little woman. Now, when

Rolissa chided dear Flora for her worries, the tattered little wren fluffed her feathers and reminded her charge that she was well-known as a discerning person. That bit of information never failed to send the young lady sailing from the room, frustrated. It would hardly do to remark that if Lord Amberly truly believed his words, he *too* was bird-witted.

By the time, nearly a fortnight later, that they attended a theatre party, London had grown used to seeing the two families together. The play was well done and left them in a convivial mood. Later, nothing could have been more pleasant than the light supper Lord Ondridge had bespoken at Grillion's. He was in an amiable mood, and with Squire Norten, Mr. Jamison, and the Honourable Mr. Jack Sayers engaging the attentions of the other ladies, he set himself to be particularly charming to Rolissa. As he leaned back in his chair, his entire attention was on her; he idly fingered his quizzing glass as they discussed the play and Kendall's performance. His voice, soft and low, held a caressing quality that Rolissa had not before heard in it.

Rolissa found herself unaccountably shy. Looking into the earl's dark eyes, for once soft and tender, she had to force light conversation over a palpitating heart.

Again that night she dreamed of him, of his broad shoulders as he leaned forward, pouring another glass of champagne. The gentle brushing of his lips on the back of her hand became, in her dream, a passionate embrace that brought her wide awake, leaving her with a longing she had never before known.

The following day she was dressed and waiting when he came with his phaeton to take her riding in the park. They had hardly entered the drive by the Serpentine when they passed two matrons who, with better birth than manners, stared at them. Rolissa gazed up at the treetops, trying to preserve her composure.

"Would it help, do you think, if we should stop and strike a pose?" Ondridge asked, throwing her a look of amusement.

"Odious women," Rolissa muttered. Without her own lively sense of humour, which, most fortunately, the earl shared, she would have been unable to bear what she could only consider rudeness of the first water. In her present frame of mind, she said as much.

"I declare, I am persuaded that such business shall drive me back to Northumberland. Where will it all end?"

"I would think that is obvious," Ondridge replied, tipping his hat to an acquaintance on the walk. "I have no doubt the hourly expectation is that I will call on Lord Amberly—a courtesy, since, while he is head of the family, you are not under the care of a guardian."

Rolissa coloured with embarrassment. It took no high degree of perception to realise that she had unthinkingly raised a topic most unbecoming in her. She went hot and cold, certain he must interpret her question as a prompting that he should declare himself. As if her memory deliberately wished to add to her burden, the dream that had awakened her the night before suddenly loomed large in her mind. Partly from her discomfiture in having brought up the subject, and partly from the fear that his refusal would be shattering, she tried to pass it off with a witticism.

"But I w-wish you will n-not," she stammered, tossing her head playfully as he turned a surprised expression upon her. "I am persuaded I have never seen Lady Jennie and Miss Smathers in such fine fettle since they are all so decided on the course of action we are considered to be taking. Y-you cannot, without knowing her from before, guess the difference in my companion, who supposed herself to be of indifferent health, but who is blooming under the rigours of her new social activities." She was chattering, she knew, but her tongue seemed suddenly converted to a lump of lead as she viewed the change in his expression. A tight look had followed his surprise and before that his good humour. His reply came from between clenched teeth.

"Far be it from me to detract from the good health of Miss Smathers," he said shortly, and urged the horses to a brisk trot.

Too late, Rolissa understood that in her embarrassment, caused by emotions he could not know she felt, she had not only led him into speaking, but had thwarted him as he tried to do so. As great as was her confusion when she brought the circumstances about, there was more in trying to discover a method of overcoming it. Where, she wondered desperately, was that glib tongue that always surfaced when she was with Tully and Jamie? With those two worthy friends, her heart was not in her mouth, a circumstance that made explanations difficult, if not impossible.

But she was to be allowed little chance. They were at that time approaching Marble Arch, and it was only minutes before they drew to a halt before Barnstowe House on Brooke Street. With a punctilious courtesy, he handed her down from the carriage and saw her to the door, promptly opened by a footman. With a short "My gratitude for your company," he was on his way again.

That evening Rolissa and Lady Jennie were engaged to attend a ball on Curzon Street. When the younger lady descended the stair, Lady Jennie was marching back and forth across the entrance hall, her impatience evident by the way the footman and the butler hovered anxiously in the rear of the passage, well out of the way of their employer.

The delay, as all the household was aware, was because of the young lady's sudden niceness in the choice of her attire. A dozen gowns had been accepted and rejected. Four had actually been donned before she settled, long after they were due at the ball, on an Indian mull muslin in a deep rose, overdraped with creamy Belgian lace. The dark curls that required very little help from the crimping iron were caught back in a ribbon that exactly matched the dress, and her dresser, worn to exasperation by Rolissa's fussiness, had roused herself to tie it in an intricate and becoming bow over her left temple.

Rolissa's efforts were not unnoticed as she entered the ballroom. The frankly admiring looks from a number of gentlemen and, even more rewarding, the measuring gazes of several young females and their ambitious mamas, told her her time had not been wasted.

She had only left her hostess when she was accosted by Lord Tulane and Mr. Jamison, who adroitly thwarted Mr. Boscomb's attempt to reach her first.

"Save me," Jamie begged. "My mentor is finding fault with me as usual, and you see me in a desperate case. When one is set down by a fellow so lacking in wit as to wear such a coat—" he flicked his handkerchief at the dark blue satin affected that evening by Tully— "well, I am blue-deviled, I can tell you."

Both gentlemen seemed uncommonly agitated, and Rolissa wondered what could have occurred to overset them, but it was not within the bounds of good manners for her to pry into their private affairs, so she refrained from asking. Instead, she joined the game.

"Poor Jamie," she crooned. "How should I do battle in your behalf?"

"By taking the floor with me, my lady," he said, as he made a tardy leg and took her arm, leading her away while Tully was still trying to make his bow.

"Why, you odious creature." She laughed as she looked over her shoulder to see Tully, momentarily holding his pose as he bowed to the vacant spot in front of him. "To do the terrible to your friend may be fine for you, but I'm persuaded you will give me a reputation for being a sad romp. And why are you and Tully not attending Miss Marchlin and Miss Singer?"

Jamie shook his head mournfully. "Alas, the love of my life has more affection for duty than for me." At Rolissa's enquiring look, he explained. "Her mother has been ill, and she has returned home again to be with her. As for Miss Singer, well, she has a very shrewd aunt. Until Tully shows positive signs of coming up to scratch, the dragon will not allow him to more than do the occasional pretty."

"Very correct," Rolissa replied, "but if Tully is in truth developing a *tendre,* it must be hard on him."

Mr. Jamison led her to the end of the room and secured a place in a just-forming set. Since their position caused them to face the wall, Rolissa was not given an opportunity to see if any of her acquaintances were attending that evening and Jamie's conversation kept her from looking around. He reverted to his playful complaints about Tully.

"You renew my courage, my lady. My mentor had quite convinced me no lady would lower herself to take the floor with me, you know. Your acceptance must build my self-esteem."

"Build yours, sir, or reduce mine?" Rolissa asked, her eyes sparkling. "If Tully is correct, indeed, how my own consequence must be lowered."

"Ah—but that is not the case at all!" Jamie gave every pretence of being profoundly shocked. "When the most beautiful and desirable female to grace London consents to be a gentleman's partner, it must be *he* who is raised to *her* heights. She can never be lowered, just as while we may be illuminated by the sun, we cannot dim it by standing in its brilliance."

"Fie, sir, are you trying to turn my head?" She affected a simper and looked away. She would have preferred a more clever retort, but her wit was lost in her confusion. What she most enjoyed about the three-way friendship was the lack of flowery compliments and courting attitude. Her times with Jamie and Tully had been made up of long rollicking games of wit, and such compliments that came her way were either ridiculous parodies of the inane praise she received from her duller suitors or had been couched in terms that gave set-downs to her that were quite the equal of those the gentlemen traded between themselves.

As the dance ended, Jamie heaved a deep, regretful sigh. "All too short, and I shall only have one other opportunity. If you will be good enough to keep the quadrille for me, it will put Tully out of sorts all evening." He led her back in the direction of the entrance, where they had left Tully and where Lady Jennie was still in conversation with their hostess.

"Of course, sir, if that is what you truly wish," she replied as she strolled along at his side. She was surprised to see him look over his shoulder, give a start, and abruptly whirl her around to face a gentleman who stood leaning against the wall.

"You haven't met Tommy!" Jamie announced with an air suspiciously akin to desperate animation. The gentleman they faced had been lounging against the wainscoting as he surveyed the room, but he came to a sudden surprised attention. Rolissa saw he was nearly as tall as the lanky Mr. Jamison, but of a more elegant figure. His clothing carried that unmistakable air of Paris fashion, and Rolissa wondered how such a presentable gentleman could be standing alone at a party where mamas with marriageable daughters abounded.

As startled as the gentleman may have been, he recollected himself to bow gracefully over Rolissa's hand. Once the introductions were over, she learned by the desultory conversation that Tommy, the Earl of Plythford, was only newly arrived in London and attending what, until that moment, he considered a very boring affair only to please his aunt, the hostess.

"Been on the Continent," Jamie said, reaching out to finger the fine material that made up the earl's evening coat.

"Have to see a bit of the world, you know." Plythford gave a low laugh and a glance at Jamie that bespoke words clearly not meant for Rolissa to understand.

"Yes, I gather it is an education," Jamie agreed, with the hint of a grin.

Rolissa's gaze strayed as she wondered what their silent messages might mean, and she was giving the matter some thought when a more urgent matter claimed her attention. Mr. Boscomb was making his way in her direction, and so purposeful were his movements, so censorious was his expression, that Rolissa did not trust herself to be in his company, lest she lose all patience and give him a set-down in no uncertain terms. She pointed out as much to Jamie.

"Good God!" Jamie exclaimed at Boscomb's determined progress. "Tommy, do yourself the great honour of leading the fair lady onto the floor and away from that fustian idiot. But do keep her at this end of the room where Tully can find her, or it will be bellows to mend with me. He told me to bring her back before her court catches up with her."

"Why, certainly, sir, if the lady will allow me."

As Jamie's arm left hers, Tommy's immediately took its place and she was summarily moved onto the dance floor. Hardly the speed of good manners when she had not actually been consulted, but the desire to escape Mr. Boscomb was too strong for her to make any objection. Any she might have made was forestalled by the gaze Lord Plythford was giving her; she could only consider it a humourous speculation.

"Lady Rolissa Amberly." Plythford spoke her name as if it surprised him. As they moved into a set his expression changed and she was reminded, most uncomfortably, of a cat eyeing a mouse. "I wonder what possessed Jamie to give you into *my* hands?"

"I beg pardon, sir?" The discomfort Rolissa felt at his enquiring but triumphant look was replaced by surprise. "I wasn't aware that one dance put me in anyone's *hands.*"

His chuckle was disquieting. "In that remark, ma'am, I perceive a set-down. Can it be that my reputation has faded during my exile?"

Though she was still without any exact knowledge of his offences, the oblique looks that had passed between Plythford and Jamie took on meaning. Rolissa now knew herself to be partnered by some notorious rake. Since her only experience of the breed had been in romantic novels, she was fascinated, not only that she had met him, but that *he* had mentioned his unsavoury reputation. Rolissa took refuge in the type of wit that characterised her conversation with Jamie and Tully.

"Forgive me. I have been much out of the city, else I would have known of it, I'm sure. What a shame, since you have only just arrived back in England, that one of the first females you meet should be so ignorant. Will I be regaled with tales, or are they not fit for a lady's ears?"

Plythford laughed outright. "I should have known. If Jamie sought your company, you had to be a right one. Make no mistake, you will doubtless have your ears boxed by your chaperone for even taking the floor with me. By tomorrow my every sorry deed will be told you by half the town, so be prepared to cut me the next time we meet."

Through all this Rolissa kept her face carefully innocent of all mirth. "Will you advise me on just how to go about it? I mean, if you are such a rogue that many are likely to cut you, you must be an expert on how such things are most gracefully done. I've had so little experience at it, you see, and it would not do to be awkward."

Plythford was clearly struggling between astonishment, laughter, and a brave attempt at looking thoughtful. He seemed to give the matter some consideration before answering.

"A good long stare without expression is best, I think. Personally, I consider cutting, by the simple expedient of pretending not to see one, a cowardly method, and it can be misinterpreted. It could be considered not a cut at all, but a matter of being overlooked in the press of people." He frowned, and then his face lit with an engaging smile. "That's quite as lowering, I think. After working very hard to gain stature in a certain direction, to have it go completely unnoticed is certainly a set-down."

Between the attentions of Jamie and Plythford, Rolissa still had not had the opportunity to see how many of her acquaintances were present, so when the dance ended, and Plythford was escorting her back to Jamie and Tully, she glanced around. They had nearly come up to her two friends, who were leaning against the wall, when her gaze lit on Ondridge. He was walking with Lady Handing as he led her back to her seat. He was bending over and giving her his entire attention.

Rolissa glanced away quickly, but she felt as though the floor had moved under her. She had doubtless made a misstep, because Plythford tightened his grip on her arm. His eyes lit immediately on the reason for her loss of composure, and she wondered how much talk there must be, if even a new arrival in London was aware of her embarrassment.

As she turned her face away from Ondridge and Lady Handing, she saw the distress in the eyes of Tully and Jamie. A rush of affection for them swelled in her, almost equal with her pain. She realised now that all their machinations had been an effort to keep her from grief. The shock of seeing Ondridge again paying his attentions to the widow had thrown her into a misery, and she made no attempt at conversation. But once more Jamie and Tully came to her rescue. The sudden eruption of an argument over cravats was lengthy, witty, and left no opportunity for her to enter on either gentleman's side.

In between the barbs that Jamie and Tully were throwing at each other, it was plain that Lord Tulane was not at all pleased with Rolissa's last dancing partner. Plythford, quite aware of the other's disapproval, exchanged a few comments with Jamie and bowed over Rolissa's hand, holding it too long, for the edification, clearly, of the frowning viscount. Then, giving Tully a sardonic smile, he strolled off to take up his position against the wall again.

Tully was just taking Rolissa's arm to lead her onto the floor when they were suddenly accosted by a grim-faced Lord Ondridge. With a curt nod to his cousin, he took Rolissa's arm. Without even the courtesy of requesting permission, he swirled her out into a waltz.

"I think you should take greater care in choosing whose partnership you accept," he said curtly.

"You object to Tully?" She looked up innocently, deliberately mistaking his meaning.

"Plythford," Ondridge snapped. "Being seen in his company will do you no good at all."

Rolissa could not but feel indignant. "I doubt it was noticed. Most seemed too busy about their own pursuits to be aware of anyone else." She bit her lip, afraid he would recognise the jealousy in her words for what it truly was.

The earl was too angry to notice. "If you reconsider, you will think better of that statement. Hardly a person in this room failed to remark that you were dancing with the greatest rogue to grace the city in a decade."

After his attentions to the widow, Rolissa thought it the height of impertinence that he should call her to task for her dancing partner. True, an unexceptionable person like Lady Handing only compared with a rogue in her own eyes, so she could hardly give vent to her intimate feelings. She was determined that Ondridge's remarks would not bring out in her another occasion for losing her temper. Instead, she looked up at him with every appearance of fascination.

"Oh, *is* he a rogue? And *I* was singled out for his attentions? That must be a compliment of no mean order—do consider, he must have *such* experience, which undoubtedly makes him a discerning person."

"I can assure you his tastes—I can assure you a gentleman who loses his reputation does so because in most instances his tastes are not at all nice."

"Oh, I take it *you* think he chose to dance with me out of pity, or because no one else was desperate enough to accept him?"

Ondridge's reply was frosty. "Because of your fortune—that I can assure you."

"Are you saying no gentleman of taste would lead me out except that I have a fortune?" Rolissa asked slowly, as if she dispassionately considered a weighty problem. "In that case, should I not desire to attend some engagement, do you think I could send my man of business? Would the gentlemen be as willing to dance with him?"

"Your levity is neither becoming nor appreciated."

"Never levity, sir. Since you have been so kind as to interest yourself in my affairs, I most earnestly seek advice. Since you yourself have led me on the floor, I thought you might be able to enlighten me."

After one final glare, Lord Ondridge raised his head and addressed no other words to her. When the dance was finished, he led her back again to where Jamie and Tully were, as usual, carrying on one of their interminable arguments. Ondridge nodded curtly to Jamie and addressed himself to Tully.

"Do you still mean to go with me to Sussex?"

"What?" Tully looked surprised. "I thought you meant to stay in town for a bit."

"Tomorrow morning I am on my way. If you intend to keep an eye on your expectations, you had best be ready."

Tully's head jerked up, the fire in his eyes as fierce as the look he received. "Perhaps I had better," he said quietly, his voice silky smooth. "I will wait on you at eleven o'clock."

"You will wait on me at eight, or find no one in residence but my mother," Ondridge announced, and with a short bow to Rolissa he strode away.

Rolissa kept her back turned as he crossed the room, determined that the *ton* would not see her wearing the willow. She gazed at Jamie and Tully, and was interested in their reactions. There was still some fire in Tully's eyes, but it was lost as he, too, looked at Jamie. He had ignored the sparks between Ondridge and Tully, and was still wearing the pleased expression that he had assumed when the earl led Rolissa onto the floor. Of the three, only he seemed to be gratified by the encounter. The look on his face was one of satisfaction, causing Tully to lose his anger and grin.

For her part, Rolissa could put no faith in their interpretation of the argument she had had with the earl. They thought he was jealous, she knew, but, unlike the gentlemen, she could not think it boded well for the connexion that had suddenly become so important in her life. Her spirits dropped again when she saw Carson leading the widow into the small salon for refreshments.

= 6 =

IN THE WEEK that followed, Rolissa was kept busy with a whirl of shopping and social activities. Miss Smathers, who abjured evening engagements now that Ondridge was no longer an active member of their society, was pressed into service for the young lady's shopping excursions and morning visits. Rolissa kept herself occupied with a constancy meant to keep the Earl of Ondridge from her mind.

Miss Smathers's relief that Lord Ondridge had absented himself from town gave way to a fresh worry that afternoon. Lord Amberly, who only that morning had been to Hatcher's in search of a book, came back much concerned. At luncheon, with the hesitation a peaceful man feels when he's aware his words may cause a storm of emotion among the women in the household, he broached the subject of Rolissa's meeting with Plythford. He assured her that he meant to throw no spoke in her enjoyment, but did she fully understand the meaning of the man's reputation? Of the danger he could present? He was brought up short by Lady Jennie's more placid viewpoint.

"Oh, I'll admit the boy was up to all the rigs a few years ago," she acknowledged. "But his reputation is not as black as he and Carson painted it. Mark my words, he'll be received everywhere. Silly young fool had a habit of running off with heiresses. Did it twice and didn't succeed either time."

"Who were they?" Rolissa asked, fascinated. The stories told to her by Miss Smathers when she was a child brought out her curiosity even while she thought the idea repulsive.

"No one ever knew. Their families kept it as quiet as possible. Word leaked out about him, but give him credit, he don't bandy their names about."

Miss Smathers was in no way mollified by the gentleman's discretion after the fact. "Jennie, you see he stays away from Rolissa," she demanded. Her concern had found a new target and she looked to Lord Amberly for support, but having brought up the issue, he appeared hesitant to add fuel to what might prove to be an emotional conflagration.

"Stuff!" Lady Jennie snorted. "Must have grown out of that nonsense long ago. Never thought his pockets were completely to let, and if he was interested in a Smithfield bargain, he'd be leg-shackled by now. Two years ago he had an heiress panting after him—good-looking girl, too—that Mary Ann Thingummy—you know, Lady Carrington's niece. Nothing the family could do, she would have him, only he suddenly pulled back. Never came up to scratch. And the girl was as rich as the Golden Ball. Nobody could understand it."

"Rolissa, you must still be on your guard," Miss Smathers insisted, not truly calmed by Lady Jennie's explanations. In the privacy of Rolissa's bedchamber, she had often given her charge the opinion that living so long in London had made their hostess blind to the dangers that lay in wait for a young woman in her first season.

At their numerous social engagements, Rolissa was extremely grateful to Jamie for his attempts to lighten her days. He was an excellent tonic for her spirits, and he gave her an account of the very real set-down he received from Tully when, unable to think of any other way to keep her from seeing Ondridge with the widow, he had introduced her to Lord Plythford.

"Poor boy." Rolissa had laughed at him, using Tully's most common term for the tall, lanky man. "You have suffered much in my behalf."

"So has Ondridge," he said, laughing. "Never saw him so high in the bows."

Lord Ondridge had been away a sennight when Rolissa's busy schedule was momentarily halted by a rainy morning. Breakfast was over, and coffee was being served in the yellow drawing room. Lord Amberly had pulled a chair to a Pembroke table and was writing some notes, and Miss Smathers was occupied with her interminable mending, while Rolissa flipped the pages of a fashion book. Lady Jennie was sitting at her escritoire, sorting through the post. She threw out an occasional bit of information as she read the invitations, inquiring of Rolissa if she cared to attend this or that engagement.

"I declare, you will run the girl into a decline," Miss Smathers complained.

"Bosh, not everyone is as feeble as you, Flora," Lady Jennie returned. "Though I don't think much of Lady Oberford's gatherings. Dashed shabby way she has of doing things." While she was speaking, a footman entered and handed her a note. "He wants to see Rolissa?"

"If it is a he, then most assuredly he wants to see Rolissa." Lord Amberly smiled as he folded his notes. "I'll take myself off to the library."

"Put off your book for a bit, Henry," Lady Jennie said with a solemnity so alien to her blustering nature that three heads came up, sensing something untoward in the making. "Unless I'm much mistaken, Rolissa, you still favor Stearns and Miller as your solicitors?"

"Of course," replied the young lady, putting aside the fashion magazine. "Father employed them exclusively, and I saw no reason to change."

"Then I think you had better stay, Henry. A solicitor by the name of Knowles wants to see Rolissa, and I cannot like it when strangers undertake to speak of legal business."

"Then it might be best if he saw Stearns and Miller," Henry said. Legalities are not my long suit—"

But Henry had no time to escape, for while Lady Jennie had first requested him to stay, she had gestured to the footman to show the visitor into the salon, and he was just entering.

Rolissa looked up to see a large, heavy gentleman. He was dressed in the proper attire for a morning visit, but it was obvious that he had never had the benefit of a London tailor. He had the air of the shires about him, and would have appeared more at home at a hunt than in a London drawing room. To the young lady's mind, a mantle of undue gravity seemed to lay uneasily on his shoulders. His voice was hushed as the introductions were made, and as he took a seat indicated by Lady Jennie, he looked at each in turn with a mournful expression. When he spoke, his voice was almost a whisper.

"Do forgive me for interrupting on this most painful occasion, but as I said in my note, I am only in town for a few hours, and I took the liberty of coming to offer my condolences and get what instructions Lady Rolissa saw fit to give me."

The four listeners at first blinked at the ambiguity of his opening statement. Both Lord Amberly and Rolissa were still silent, but Lady Jennie and Miss Smathers both caught on the key words. While the frail gentlewoman set up a moan of despair, Lady Jennie came to the point in her forthright manner.

"Who died?"

Mr. Knowles found it was his turn to blink, and seemed to be in some consternation. "Can it be the word has not reached London? Oh, dear, how painful it is to bring such news. It is, I fear, my sad duty to tell you the Marquess of Letton, together with his wife and their twin sons, have met with a fatal accident."

"Whippy?" Lady Jennie demanded, not believing what she was hearing.

Miss Smathers set up a wail. "The family is cursed!"

Rolissa stared at the solicitor, trying to take in what she had heard. John Whipple, the Marquess of Letton, had been a distant relative, but one she had never seen. Moreover, she thought of him not as a member of the family as much as a friend and correspondent of her father's. They had not visited within her memory, but they had exchanged frequent and lengthy letters.

For a few moments the scene was one of incongruity. Lord Amberly still stared at the solicitor as though he could not quite take in what had been said. Rolissa, feeling a wash of sadness, thinking of how the news would have affected her father if he had still lived, was unable to sit still. Suddenly the pain of her parent's death was back again, and she rose abruptly, and took to pacing to and fro behind the confidante on which she had been seated.

Miss Smathers, feeling it incumbent on her, as the member of the family most known for her sensibility, to show proper feelings, continued to wail and fall prostrate on the confidante so recently vacated by Rolissa. All her evidence of swooning abruptly left her, however, when her hostess, impatient with the display, declared she would have one of the footmen cart the silly goose away. Faced with a choice of maintaining her theatrics, thereby missing the rest of the interview with Mr. Knowles, or bringing her hysterics to an immediate halt, the little woman sat up and sniffed loudly into her handkerchief, over which she watched the other occupants with a birdlike gaze.

"It's hard to believe," Lord Amberly murmured. "We were at school together. One's friends start going, and it's as if one has lost part of himself." Seeing her cousin so visibly shaken, Rolissa forced her own pain down and went to sit by him.

"How did it happen?" Lady Jennie asked when a measure of peace had been restored.

Mr. Knowles sighed, ran a finger around his neckcloth in his discomfort, and gave Miss Smathers a wary glance. Clearly, he was afraid his news might overset her again, but faced with the imposing stare of Lady Jennie, whose bulk added to her authority, he took a deep breath and started his story.

"Ah—a terrible ending for a day so full of promise for a happy family," he moaned. "The marquess was planning to visit a neighbour that morning to discuss the purchase of a hunter, I understand. The marchioness was with him—they started out alone—we assume he encountered the nurse and the children on the grounds and took them up in the carriage. The road along the cliffs was hazardous, but not dangerous to one of his ability with horses, you understand. However, a wheel came off the carriage at a most unfortunate place, leaving the vehicle teetering on the edge of the cliff. The occupants were thrown over—" He paused, casting another doubtful look at Miss Smathers, and was reassured by the lack of sniffing coming from behind the handkerchief.

"They found the marquess and his lady washed up on the shore the next morning, but the twins and the nurse—" He spread his hands, a gesture that explained the rest.

Miss Smathers started to moan, but one sharp look from Lady Jennie silenced her.

"You *assume* they took the children in the carriage?" Rolissa found it hard to accept the death of two small children—the twins had been nearly two.

"Very good point," Lady Jennie observed. "Why, since their bodies weren't found?"

"Lord Letton was very fond of the boys and often took them up in the carriage. No reflection on him, of course, but local gossip said the nurse often complained that his love of being with the boys kept them from a regular schedule. That, added to the fact that neither the nurse nor the children have been seen since, and the tale becomes too painfully clear. We kept hoping we were wrong, but no other answer is forthcoming."

"Poor little blighters," Henry said, and raised a suddenly shaking hand to his forehead. He had paled alarmingly.

"Well." Lady Jennie sat back, her hands braced against the chair arms. "So Whippy bought it. Never liked him above half, myself. Always too high in the instep. But sorry about his family. Who gets the title and his fortune?"

Such blunt speaking brought out a small screech from Miss Smathers, and a shocked look from the visiting solicitor. Rolissa, now past the pain the news had brought her, repressed a smile at her aunt's forthright question.

Mr. Knowles seemed to have trouble catching his breath, but he pulled himself together and indicated the thin portmanteau at his side, the type used by men of business to carry papers.

"That is my reason for coming, my lady. There are two people most favourably affected by the will. The title, the entailed estates, and part of the fortune accrues to Lord Ondridge, as the nearest male relative in the line of succession, the family being quite thinned by the war and illness. The unentailed properties and a considerable part of the marquess's wealth was left to the late Lord Amberly and his heirs."

"Then Cousin Henry will benefit," Rolissa said, giving Lord Amberly a smile.

"No, my lady," Mr. Knowles interrupted. "The marquess was a gentleman of some years before he married, and his last will was made before he had taken a wife, but long after you were born. In the event he left no heirs, your name was expressly mentioned as the recipient of your father's part of the estate."

Rolissa sat quite still, dumbfounded by the news. Lord Amberly, too, looked to be quite overset, and for a moment he seemed to be fighting for breath. He sat with his mouth open, his lips working to form his words.

"I am very pleased for you, my dear," he finally managed in a quiet voice. "Jennie, I think I am too overset by the news to be of any help, and must retire to the library." So saying, he rose and walked unsteadily across the room to the door.

"Oh, the poor man." Miss Smathers hurried after him. "I, too, feel in need of rest."

Together they disappeared through the door, with the three who were still sitting watching in varying attitudes. Rolissa's eyes followed them mechanically. Her thoughts traveled back to the news that the children had been in the carriage. Shortly before her father's death, they had received word of the birth of the twins, and she remembered her father laughing over his old friend's young family.

"Just as well they left the room," Lady Jennie said, shifting her bulk and kicking off her shoes, as she was wont to do when giving serious attention to a problem. "Now we can get on with it. What is the girl to expect?"

"Aunt Jennie!" Rolissa gasped at the straightforward approach that seemed so unfeeling to her.

"Nonsense, girl. Don't *you* go missish on me. What's done is done. Being thrown into the doldrums or the vapours won't bring back Whippy or his offspring. Nothing wrong with you finding out what's yours."

"True." Mr. Knowles, fast becoming enured to Lady Jennie's lack of sentimentality, nodded in agreement. "It is best that you know your affairs. You will, of course, want your own solicitors to handle the matter, but you need to be made aware of an approximation, which is all I can give you at the moment. Altogether, in properties and investments in the funds, you may look forward to around ninety thousand pounds."

"Good heavens!" Lady Jennie was for once too astonished to resort to one of her colourful expletives, and fell back on a gentler one. In a moment she rallied and became her old practical self.

"I had no thought it would be so much," Rolissa murmured. "I must give you the direction of Stearns and Miller, my solicitors. I have no comprehension of very large amounts."

"Certainly, my lady." Mr. Knowles nodded sympathetically. "No doubt these excellent gentlemen can present it to you in a form easier to understand when the sorting out of properties is complete."

What took no great intellect to understand, Lady Jennie suggested, was that word of this addition to her already quite impressive fortune would bring every fortune hunter in England, if there were any left that had not already tried to court Rolissa. She said as much, and requested Mr. Knowles to make no mention of his visit or its purpose, hoping to keep the gossip-mongering tongues quiet for as long as possible.

Courteously refusing all offers of refreshment, Mr. Knowles took his leave. For a few minutes Lady Jennie shook her head, as if chasing away sleep or cobwebs, and then she rose with decision.

"Go shopping," she ordered her niece. "Take your abigail and look to your summer wardrobe if nothing else. Keep yourself busy until I can calm Flora down. If I don't take care, she'll try to have us all in deep mourning."

"We should at least be wearing black gloves," Rolissa said hesitantly.

"We won't," Lady Jennie retorted with some asperity. "Your come-out's been delayed too long by mourning, and I won't have it again. Devil take that Whippy!" Lady Jennie, for once shocking herself with her outburst, raised a plump hand to cover her mouth. With gimlet eyes, she peered around as if her words might have called up that denizen of the dark world.

"Aunt Jennie, shame on you!" Rolissa could not keep back a giggle of shock.

"Well, he always was inconsiderate," her aunt temporized. "Even in the time he picked to get himself killed."

"I am persuaded he did not choose it," Rolissa commented.

"We still won't go into black gloves," Lady Jennie ruled. "He was only a distant relation, after all. You never knew him, and Henry, for all his shock, is thinking about the generation, and not the man. Seems once your generation starts falling by the wayside, there's no stopping it."

Rolissa did as her aunt suggested. In the company of her maid she completed several purchases and stopped in Hatchard's to peruse the newest novel of Sir Walter Scott. It was there that she discovered Lady Jennie's excellent caution about not puffing off her new inheritance had come too late.

Rolissa was absorbed in a preliminary exploration of *Rob Roy* and had just decided to purchase it when she heard a soft male voice behind her.

"Have you been practicing your cut, ma'am?"

She turned to see Lord Plythford standing behind her, idly turning the pages of a tour book on Holland. He was dressed in riding clothes and top boots, not the usual attire for Bond Street.

She gave him a playful curtsey. "Oh, sir, you must forgive my sad manners, but the truth is, I have been without a moment to do so, and I am convinced I should not try it in public, not having assured myself of the proper method."

He continued turning the pages of the book as if unaware of her presence, but he chuckled softly. "You are, of course, forgiven. It must take a great deal of time and energy to spend *two* fortunes."

"Two, sir?" she queried with astonishment. Surely he could not be aware of the accuracy of his words. "Could you tell me what prompted that statement?"

Plythford raised his eyebrows. "Is your newest inheritance to be kept a secret? If so, I fear you're doomed to disappointment. It will be all over town by evening."

"Then, of course, there is no point in denying it to you," she said shortly, "but I would like to know how the word went about the town almost before I knew of it. It only reached me this morning."

Plythford gave her a slight, mocking bow. "My information, though at least third hand, is at your disposal. It seems your solicitor, Mr. Knowles, stayed at Grillion's last night and joined a party of cronies there. He finished the evening in Cribbs Parlour—and apparently a very garrulous fellow in his cups is the country gentleman."

"Dash it!" Rolissa exclaimed, and then her eyes widened at her own temerity and she covered her mouth with her hand. "I declare, I have been too long in the company of Aunt Jennie—oh, that's not at all the thing to say, either," she snapped in vexation as Lord Plythford laughed.

"You must think me very odd," she explained, "but it is not at all comfortable being an heiress at times. I would not like to be in want, of course, but—" How, she wondered, did she say what she felt to a man accused of being the most infamous of fortune hunters?

Plythford's smile was sympathetic. "But when a man courts you, you would like to be sure of what has attracted him?"

"Precisely," Rolissa answered, glad he had put it so succinctly.

"Then perhaps I could be of assistance." Plythford bowed, and when her eyebrows went up, he nodded solemnly. "Since by now you must know my reputation, you can have no doubt that the attraction for me is your wealth, and so could rest easy. At least I can be trusted."

Rolissa laughed. "As you say, sir, you can be trusted. I must keep that in mind."

Their conversation was cut short by the entrance into the shop of Lady Jersey and Princess Esterhazy, the latter seeking the same work that had brought Rolissa to Hatchard's.

Lord Plythford, with a thoughtfulness not to be expected from one of his reputation, had moved quickly behind a high stack of books and was engaged in a search of the shelves when the restless Lady Jersey came up to him.

"Plythford!" she said with surprise. "You dear rogue, I turn my back for a few days and you come back into town. I had no idea. But, I gather, if you will be anywhere, it would be in the company of an heiress." She laughed, casting a sly look in Rolissa's direction.

"But most assuredly, Sally," Plythford replied, bowing over her hand. "I am nothing if not assiduous in the pursuit of my career. I have just been telling Lady Rolissa that since my reputation is well-established, I am one of the few swains in London that she can trust implicitly."

"Has he really?" Lady Jersey looked at Rolissa with an impish smile.

"Indeed he has, ma'am, and I am convinced that at least *his* motives are beforehand."

The Princess Esterhazy came round the other side of the table, carrying a copy of *Rob Roy*. She looked at Rolissa with the hauteur for which she was famed.

"I cannot say, young lady, that you'd do worse with a known rake like Plythford than with the unannounced one you have most fortunately cast from your court of suitors."

Lady Jersey looked disapproving. "I thought we agreed that even if he was a little sudden, it was only bad taste."

"You and Myra Sefton agreed," the princess replied coldly. "For my part, I think for Ondridge to declare himself the Marquess of Letton before people even knew of his predecessor's death is a sign the man is far too enamoured with his own consequence—and puts more than a natural amount of importance on his possessions."

Rolissa was at the moment counting out the sum of her purchase, a practice her Aunt Jennie deplored. Now, however, Rolissa was grateful that she had something to occupy her. She felt the blood drain away from her face, and prayed she would not swoon. Fortunately, she was saved from further conversation by the entrance of her abigail. Unaware that the remarks passing back and forth between the Almack's hostesses had included her mistress, Maggie immediately began to press Rolissa to accompany her to the establishment of a particular milliner, where an extremely modish hat, and one that would just match her new promenade gown, had just been put on display.

In the confusion of Lord Plythford's leavetaking, and the urgings of her own maid, Rolissa was able to escape the shop with a bare nod to the powerful society women, and hardly noticed by them.

"Stupid thing for him to do!" Lady Jennie announced for the fifth time as they were on their way to Lady Richmond's ball that night. "Stupid thing. Wonder why he'd make such a cake of himself over another title? Just a headache, and not that much better than being an earl."

The ball was a grand crush. By the time they had waited in the tangle of carriages to reach the door, and had been standing on the grand stair in a cluster of arriving guests for nearly half an hour, Rolissa was heartily wishing they had sent their regrets.

As Plythford had warned, the news of her inheritance had reached everyone in the *ton,* and along with congratulations, she received some acid comments from some who were less plump in the pocket and resentful of it. The subject was noticeably absent in the conversation of several gentlemen who suddenly found her very attractive, though most of them had seen her regularly without undue enthusiasm at the previous social events of the season.

When Jamie was at last able to claim her hand for the quadrille, she begged him to take pity on her poor feet and her thirst.

He shook his head in disapproval. "A lady of fashion never admits to something as mundane as aching feet," he admonished her. "To chastise you for that remark I will not allow you to sit—at least not here."

"Jamie, you are a wretch," Rolissa told him, but changed her mind as he led her out onto the terrace.

The night was unseasonably warm, and taking advantage of the opportunity to show off her famous gardens, Lady Richmond had caused lanterns to be lit on the terrace and on the paths below that were reached by a stair descending from just opposite the ballroom.

It was not into the garden that Mr. Jamison took Rolissa, but to an ornately carved and gilded bench at one side of the terrace.

"Wait here and I'll get you some refreshment," he told her. "But stay in the shadows, or you'll be out on the floor before I can return."

Rolissa sat leaning against the stone of the building, enjoying the coolness at her back. Below her, she heard the light voices of several young ladies who were strolling in the garden. From the sounds, they were met by several gentlemen, and the conversation seemed to blend into a gentle drone punctuated with an occasional trill of laughter.

To her left, just beyond the bench, a narrow shaft of light fell on the smooth stone floor of the terrace from a window in the room beyond. The curtains had been opened and a window thrown back. There was a rustle of silk and voices came from the room.

"Oh, my dear, so much cooler, though I daresay we shall all die of the chill," said a gentle-voiced woman.

"Such a crush—I wish I had sent my regrets," came an answer in more strident tones.

"You are so right. I cannot know why I came," added a third voice.

"Possibly to watch Miss Marrel romping after Lord Haynes," the strident voice answered. "Lord, did you ever see a chit make such a fool of herself? What can her mother be thinking of to allow it?"

"Well, after the rout at Woreston House, I don't suppose we will see Lady Rolissa Amberly and Ondridge doing the pretty," said the third woman. "John says I'm imagining things, but I am convinced they had words—right there on the floor."

"If the child has any sense, we won't. Tying herself up with him would be cutting her own throat, and believe me, he'll be the one holding the razor—there's money to be gained by it."

"Emma, you should not say that," the soft-voiced woman spoke up. "Why, I have known Carla Talmadge these many years, and—"

"And what does that say to anything?" the strident Emma demanded. "Every cutthroat ever born had a mother."

"But to accuse Carson Talmadge is monstrous—"

"Is it? Everyone said the older brother was too bruising a rider to have fallen without good cause, and now there is Whippy. Lord, in his youth, Whippy could drive to an inch. He wouldn't drive off that road or any other."

"But it's impossible to believe that Talmadge could have had anything to do with either death. Why, he was on the Peninsula when his brother fell from that horse."

"If you had troubled to check as some others did—no, keep your frowns for those who shall remain nameless—you would know that tiger of his was in England. They say the way that cutpurse talks to Ondridge, he knows he cannot be turned off."

"I simply will not believe it of Carla's boy." The soft-voiced woman sounded adamant.

Harsh Emma gave an exclamation of impatience. "In just over a year, he has moved from an obscure army captain to a marquess, and over two deaths that are suspicious. Believe me, if that girl, with her money, is fool enough to accept him, she will be dead within a year."

"I simply will not believe that of Carla's boy—"

"Letty, you are a goose! You always were, and you always . . ."

The voices were faded by distance as Jamie, who had returned with two glasses of lemonade, took Rolissa's arm and led her away from the window where she had been sitting, too shocked, too hurt to move. Now, too numbed to object, she allowed Jamie to lead her down the stair and out into the garden. Once they reached the flagstone paths, he handed her the glass of lemonade. She drank it automatically, trying to shut away the pain caused by hearing the women's talk. She allowed Jamie to guide her steps on the flagstone paths, taking first one and then another to prevent nearing the other couples and groups who were taking the air. It was some time before she could even acknowledge his presence. Finally, she looked up at him, her eyes full of pain.

"You heard?" she asked quietly.

He nodded slightly. "Hen-witted gossip, nothing more, my dear. Pay it no heed."

"Carson could not be a murderer, could he?" she asked plaintively, like a child begging for reassurance.

"Couldn't possibly be," Jamie answered, looking out over the garden. "He wasn't anywhere near either place when the accidents happened. Take my word for it, that's all they were, accidents. It would make as much sense to say you killed your distant cousin for his money, and no one would believe that."

"They might," Rolissa said. "My father, my cousin—why not? No more hen-witted than to believe Carson would, is it? And all that talk about his tiger. What did that mean?"

Jamie shook his head. "None of it signifies. The little rodent was a thief or some such, and attached himself to Ondridge in the army. Got an uppity tongue, but he'd die for his 'captain'—that no one would deny who knows him."

"But we both had so much to gain," Rolissa murmured. "If the deaths weren't accidents, then—"

"Then nothing," Jamie said positively. "No one could doubt you, and if Carson had something like that in mind, he'd hardly let Tully travel with him—" He stared out over the garden as if he saw a disaster in the making.

Suddenly frightened, Rolissa grasped his arm, wrinkling his elegant sleeve. "Jamie, what is it?"

Jamie was obviously putting some effort into trying to relax. "Nothing. Nothing at all, just foolishness. He certainly wouldn't have anything to gain from doing Tully in. Tully inherits from him, but not the other way around—" Jamie stopped speaking, aware suddenly of what his words implied. He gazed at Rolissa, stricken. "Good God, Rolissa, pay no heed to me. It's just my foolishness. My concern for Tully. Of course Carson had nothing to do with *any* of it."

But Rolissa was no longer listening. All his assurances had been to calm her. If he had really believed them he wouldn't be concerned about his friend. The shock was wearing off and the question was looming larger and larger. Was she in love with a murderer?

=7=

IT WAS NOT to be thought exceptional that Rolissa was for days considering the conversation she had overheard at the Richmonds' ball. After the first shock of knowing that the gossip had begun in force again, she determined that she believed not one word of it, but in the back of her mind was the possibility. Every time a dark thought reared its suspicious head, she was wracked with pain that the man she had grown to love could be so suspected.

Over and over she tried to reaffirm her faith in Ondridge. He could not be guilty of the accusations levelled against him, and she was determined to ignore them all.

As determined as she was to keep a light heart, the prying eyes of the *ton* made evening gatherings a nightmare. Three things only brought her consolation. The constant support of Jamie, the occasional company of Lord Plythford, and the absence of Mr. Boscomb's attentions, which were directly due to the former's presence. The staid young man informed her privately that if she was a female wont to encourage the attentions of such a gentleman, he saw no recourse but to withdraw his suit. After the interview, she congratulated herself on keeping a straight face, since for three years it was well-known that Mr. Boscomb was also hanging after a rich wife, but his lack of address and his fustian manner rendered him so ineligible in the eyes of most of the young ladies of society that he was not considered interesting enough for gossip.

Rolissa was quick to discover that, though Plythford made much of his cuts, they were considerably less numerous than he had intimated. In fact, he was received everywhere, and even the staid hostesses of Almack's considered him an asset. Three days after Lady Richmond's ball, Rolissa saw him at a rout given by Lady Jersey. The evening was far advanced when he made a graceful leg to Lady Jennie and begged Rolissa to honour him with a dance.

Lady Jennie, never one to mince her words, raised her own quizzing glass and looked him up and down. "I should withhold my consent, you rakeshame," she said, glaring at him. "You haven't called in Brooke Street—not that I'd receive you, of course."

Plythford looked quite surprised. "Haven't you heard of my evil designs upon your niece? Now, how could you expect me to bring them about if she sees me in your company? Within half an hour she would be aware that my heart belongs to you, and that would be the end of all my expectations."

Lady Jennie drew back, her chin receding into the folds of her neck, her twinkling eyes nullifying her frown. "Get along with you! I had hopes you would learn to behave in time. I see I was wrong."

The dance was a waltz, and as they walked in the promenade before the line dissolved into swirling couples, Rolissa frowned prettily up at him.

"I see. So it is my aunt and not I who holds your heart?"

"But, of course, my dear. Those who know the indomitable Lady Jennie must either love her or shake in terror when she enters the room. Since I have an aversion to quaking—it does such terrible things to my cravat—I must needs give her my heart."

"Your heart, indeed, and if anything should make you shake, I should wish to see it—on second thought, I had better not. My goodness, there is Tully just entering. I wasn't aware he was back in town."

"Ah, the worst possible news for me." Plythford made a long face. "You know what a taking he'll fall into when he sees you in my company. Jamie will certainly get another harsh set-down."

"Oh, I think Jamie can hold his own if he wants to." Rolissa laughed, but the mirth died on her lips. Behind Tully she saw Lord Ondridge, bowing over the hand of Lady Jersey.

When Rolissa and Lord Plythford left the floor and returned to where Lady Jennie was holding court, Viscount Tulane had already joined Jamie and was raking him down for his choice in waistcoats.

"You see!" Plythford chided Jamie, "I warned you what would happen if you wore that tasteless rag."

His remark effectively silenced Tully, who was clearly not about to travel any further on a course with the Earl of Plythford as an ally. Yet he could hardly switch sides. Rolissa swallowed her laugh as he drew himself up in what she had come to think of as a "Mr. Boscomb puff" and refused to be drawn out.

Plythford bowed again over Lady Jennie's hand and was about to take his leave when Lady Carla came rushing up, her childishly transparent expression full of what she considered her brilliant strategy. By joining Lady Jennie's group, she was forcing her son to come into Rolissa's presence in order to greet his mother.

Rolissa felt increasingly animated from the moment she became aware that Carson was present. The warmth of her cheeks warned her of her heightened colour, her wit sharpened, and a slight raising of Plythford's eyebrows as he appraised her warned her that he had noticed the sparkle in her eyes. But she could feel her anticipation ebb as she realised the significance of Lady Carla's approach. Ondridge was not racing to her side. Indeed, he would only be forced into her presence by the necessity of greeting his mama.

Pain and frustration mingled in her bosom, making her breathing difficult. The strategy of Lady Carla's plan struck Rolissa and Plythford at the same time. Their eyes met, his amused, hers veiled to cover her distress. Coolly, Plythford leaned forward to favor Rolissa with a quiet comment.

"I think we are in for a game of chess, and Lady Carla has made the first move of the evening." As she raised her eyes to meet his again, he smiled. "An interesting opening gambit."

Rolissa was trying to think of an answer when she saw Ondridge stop on his way across the floor, making a bow to Lady Handing. She bit her lip and looked defiantly up at Plythford, but before she could speak, Jamie stepped forward, opening his snuff box, offering it to Plythford. That he had overheard the lord's quiet remarks, there was no doubt.

"And the second move is in the manner of a check," he said.

"I am of the opinion that I must have some lemonade," Rolissa announced, fluttering her fan to cool her cheeks, flushed with embarrassment and pain.

"And the queen makes a diagonal move." Plythford grinned down at her, offering his arm. "Will a knight join the rook and the queen?" he asked Jamie.

"With only a little side-stepping on my part," Jamie replied, taking Rolissa's other arm. Out of the corner of her eye, Rolissa saw Ondridge check his pace as he crossed the floor, and suddenly turn back to Lady Handing.

Let him go, she thought, raising her chin. Who wants a man who could turn from one woman to another as fast as a windcock in a storm?

Her determination to greet Ondridge coolly when she reentered the main salon suffered a setback. She was forced to call on every ounce of her willpower to approach the area where Lady Jennie and Lady Carla were still together. Lady Jennie was in conversation with Tully, and the dowager countess was giving her attention to Lady Handing, who was standing at Ondridge's side. Lady Carla's eyes were childishly wide, her concern over the presence, not only of Lord Plythford, whom she considered a rival of her son's, but also of Lady Handing, was so apparent that she was drawing amused glances from every side.

Knowing the sweet, featherheaded woman to be in a misery equaling her own, Rolissa attempted to put aside her feelings and made an effort to smooth the difficult situation. It was with a bright, welcoming smile that she returned his greeting. The delighted look this brought to Lady Carla's face showed that Rolissa had pulled off her deception.

"And I beg leave to present Lady Handing," Lord Ondridge said, introducing the two younger women.

Rolissa, never one disposed to dislike without just cause, was able to offer a more genuine smile to the young widow. It was the first time Rolissa had been in close proximity to the female upon whom Lord Ondridge had lavished so much attention, and she noted that the aura of serenity, apparent even from a distance, was much more evident when one was near her. She was a lady whose lips tended to curve into sweetness, even when in repose, but other than her gentle demeanour, there was nothing about her that could be called beautiful. No single feature was so predominant as to mar her looks; she was simply a rather plain person, and no effort with hairstyles or clothing was resorted to in order to enhance her appearance.

"Lady Rolissa." She smiled, holding out her hand. "I am indeed glad to meet you. I do believe our fathers were friends in their youth."

When Rolissa felt she had done her best to relieve Lady Carla's mind, she allowed Jamie to take her in to supper, accompanied by Tully and Miss Singer. With their pleasant company and with numerous dancing partners, she was able to keep her spirits up for the rest of the evening. It was not until she had returned home and retired for the night that melancholy crept over her and lay like a heavy covering. She was some time awake, and when sleep did come it was full of dreams that left her dull and listless in the morning.

After breakfast she dressed to accompany her aunt on a morning visit and was awaiting Lady Jennie in the yellow drawing room when one of the servants entered, asking if she was in to the Marquess of Letton.

Rolissa was at first confused. Then it occurred to her that her visitor was Carson Talmadge, using his new title. A thrill of pleasure refused to be held back, and as she instructed the footman to show him in, her voice trembled with her emotion. Perhaps, without so many others around, she could smooth out the problems her quick tongue had caused. He had been on the point of making her an offer, so he must care.

Forgetting all the hurts they had given each other, she rushed to the mirror over the mantel and straightened her riband and gave an additional puff to her full short sleeves. Then she took a seat and waited, but even as she did, she saw her hands shaking in her lap. That would never do, she decided, clutching them together tightly. Better that she keep a tight hold on her emotions and let him make the first step, since she could not trust herself.

As he entered and came forward to bow over her hand, she thought no man in England had such perfect form and address when he wanted to show it, but his very formality put her off. The stiffness he evidenced so far outweighed that of their first encounter that she was completely dismayed.

"Marquess," she said primly, trying to hide her disappointment. "I must remember that."

Her words appeared to give him pause, but the check was only of momentary duration. He waited until she asked him to be seated.

"Now, sir, is there some way I can assist you?" she asked, knowing as she spoke that in her effort to show him a similar cool attitude, she was ruining any chance of a reconciliation. Only the slightest flicker of his eyelids showed that her attitude was even noticed.

"I assume Mr. Knowles has visited you?" His voice was as cold as that of a stranger who wishes to remain so.

"The solicitor? Yes, he has." What, she wondered, could that have to do with him?

"Then you are doubtless aware that you and I together have inherited. Have you made any close investigation into the properties and the fortune involved?"

Rolissa felt her eyes widen in astonishment. While she was still wondering if she should not at least don black gloves, he was surely not expecting her to be so unfeeling as simply to devote her mind to the gains. The idea was repugnant to her.

"I have not," she replied icily, with more calmness in her voice than she believed possible. Her reaction must have been quite evident, however, because his eyes narrowed. The look she received in turn was as cold as her voice had been.

"I am aware already of society's opinion of me for not delaying in taking what is mine—but judging from your greeting, you feel the same way about the additional inheritance." He had been sitting with one buff-clad knee over the other, but he shifted, putting both feet on the floor.

"What you don't seem to realise is that Whippy's death didn't stop the life that goes on within the bounds of that land, but inaction on our part will kill it, too. If the tenants are to remain, they must be told. If they continue to put in crops, which are their livelihoods, they have to be informed they will be keeping their farms. Their planning can't wait for your convenience or a proper time of mourning."

"No—of course, you are right," Rolissa murmured, at once chastised, not by his heated speech as much as by her own good sense when he pointed out the obvious.

"It isn't a condition most women would have any reason to think about," he said quietly. There seemed, she thought, to be no anger in him. He seemed to be feigning a deliberate coldness, but his reason for such an unfathomable attitude eluded her.

"Unless you have experience in handling large and varied properties." he continued, "it's a difficult undertaking, at best."

"I am persuaded my man of business can cope . . ." Rolissa let her words trail off, wondering if she would be required to hire an assistant for him or just what would be necessary. At the moment, she was too caught up with her emotions to give practical matters any concentration. He had launched into a lengthy dissertation, sounding exactly like a man of business.

"Your man needn't be bothered with the task at all if you will entertain my proposal," he said. "The will sounds clear-cut, as if there was a dividing line down the middle and your share was on one side of a fence and mine on the other. Unfortunately, that is far from the truth. We two have inherited land that has run side by side for generations. The investment of the incomes has been run together, and it will be the devil's own task to separate them. Without cooperation, we can scare off the good tenants, allow the properties to run down, and lose income while we decide who owns what. I think you should consider letting me control all of the Letton estates until it can be sorted out."

"You are willing to assume a task of that size?" Rolissa asked, buying time while she thought about his staggering suggestion.

"Someone has to, to reassure the tenants, see to the repairs. Until everything is sorted out, two people trying to manage it are going to cause difficulties and delays."

It suddenly crossed Rolissa's mind that he was speaking of far more than just the tenants. If she had understood Mr. Knowles correctly, much of her inheritance was in investments, mostly in the funds, and did not need to be considered in relation to seasons and planting.

As if time had dissolved, she seemed to be back again on that terrace of Richmond House, where through the window came the damning gossip about Carson Talmadge. She had been certain the talk was completely without foundation, but the attitude he was displaying was forcing doubts in her mind again. How could he be so unfeeling, so grasping?

Had he been observing her closely, he would have noticed that something was definitely wrong, but he was reaching in his pocket, pulling out a folded paper.

"I have had my solicitor draw up this agreement, and if you will sign it, it will relieve you of any worries until all these matters are sorted out. It allows me to manage for two years—"

"I fear, sir, you have been wasting both your time and his," Rolissa announced, keeping her voice under control only with considerable effort. "I cannot think how you would have been so remiss in judging me that you would have thought I would allow the management of my properties out of my own hands."

His cold, impersonal attitude fell away, and Rolissa could see the· rage in his eyes. For a moment, she felt a twinge of fear of this seeming stranger who sat across from her.

At that moment the door opened and Lord Amberly advanced a few paces into the room before observing the uncommon attitudes of the two occupants. Rolissa knew he noticed the anger and trepidation in her expression. Concern showed upon his own visage.

"My dear, are you quite all right?"

"Of course, Henry," Rolissa answered him, her voice trembling with emotion. "The *marquess*," she continued, emphasizing the title, "has just made me a most *interesting* offer."

Lord Amberly could not be faulted for the look of perplexity he assumed. Obviously, the phrase "interesting offer" carried a connotation not normally associated with those words. There was certainly nothing romantic in the attitude of the two people in the room, nor did Henry make the mistake of suspecting that Carson would offer Rolissa a carte blanche.

"Interesting offer?" he queried, taking several tentative steps toward them, as if not sure of his ground.

"Oh, most assuredly," Rolissa answered. "It seems the marquess feels he should have had all the Letton properties, not just the portion left to him. I, however, do not see that it is incumbent on me to increase his holdings at the expense of myself, however altruistic he might think I should be."

Rolissa surveyed her shocked cousin and the glaring Carson Talmadge, who was by then on his feet, the folded document dangling from his fingers. His eyes blazed with rage.

"I have made no suggestion that I take the properties—your cousin here can tell you I could not do so. If you distrust me and would care to have your own man draw up what you consider a suitable agreement, it would serve the purpose just as well." He paused for a moment, as if trying to gather the rags of his own self-control.

But Rolissa, fighting her heartbreak, was past listening to reason.

Only by striking out, by staying on the offensive, could she keep any rein on herself, slight as her hold might be.

"You have had my final word, sir." She turned and strode out of the room, barely reaching her bedroom before the tears came in a storm.

Pleading a headache, Rolissa begged off the morning visit, insisting Miss Smathers should go in her place, a task that took some effort. The little woman was determined not to leave the side of her charge, fearing Carson would return, though to what purpose she had not made at all clear. Lady Jennie, a sensible woman on all points but colour, demanded Miss Smathers's company and adjured Lord Amberly to leave Rolissa in peace until she was feeling more the thing.

For Rolissa, the plea of a headache was not feigned. The product of the violent emotions that had caused her to act contrary to her usually controlled and happy nature grew worse by the minute. Fortunately for the surcease of her pain, the maid entered the room and found her sitting in a chair, her hands protecting her eyes from the light. Ignoring Lady Jennie's directive that the young lady was to be left undisturbed, she bundled Rolissa into bed and brought a dose of laudanum. The effect of the drug was enough to keep Rolissa asleep for several hours, and when she awoke she was constrained to hurry in order to have tea with the family.

Lord Amberly, Lady Jennie, and Miss Smathers were gathered in the yellow salon when she entered. Miss Smathers was at once on her feet, rushing across the room.

"My dear, are you sure you are sufficiently restored to leave your room? We were discussing sending you a tray."

Lady Jennie made an exasperated sound. "*You* were discussing it, Flora. Leave the girl alone. I won't have her made into an invalid. A wound to the self-esteem is not fatal—or permanent."

"Jennie! How can you be so unfeeling?" Miss Smathers cried in anquished accents, but Rolissa interrupted.

"I declare! If I must listen to an altercation over my supposed illness, I think I *will* go back to my room."

That was sufficient to bring both ladies to instant silence, and although she received a reproachful look from Miss Smathers, Lady

Jennie smiled into her teacup. But they had both given up a little too easily, Rolissa thought. As she watched under her lids, she noticed her robust aunt was looking slightly pale and not exhibiting her usual awesome appetite. Miss Smathers appeared even more bedraggled than was customary, but since her face lacked colour at the best of times, Rolissa could not tell from her complexion if she had suffered a loss in that direction.

But if Miss Smathers was slightly under the weather, she still had her mind soundly upon her most recent concern, and was not to be stopped when she had something she wanted to say. From her position, where she presided over the teapot, she poured Rolissa a cup of tea and then wielded the container as if the spout were the sword Excalibur, jabbing her points home.

"One thing has to be said. Rolissa has shown admirable good sense by refusing that terrible man's advances. When I think how we considered encouraging our dear girl to marrying a man that was only interested in her wealth—" She ended with a sniff, reaching for her vinaigrette. "My dear, will you ever forgive us for such a horrid thing?"

"Dear, do not, I beg of you, be a featherbrain," Rolissa answered fondly. "You had no more idea than I, I am sure. Not that I believe the stories they put about, but it is simply that we will not suit." Rolissa hoped her words were convincing to the family. They might, she knew, be true in reference to Carson Talmadge, but her pain when she discovered the reason for his visit had shown her once again her heart's direction.

"Well, you have been more intelligent than you know, and kept yourself from considerable danger," Miss Smathers retorted.

"Flora, you are a goose!" Lady Jennie expostulated. "You've let the gossip go to your head. I don't believe a word of it, and never will . . ." She paused, her voice dropping to the querulous. "What bothers me is his threat to tie up the estate."

"Tie up the estate?" Rolissa asked, puzzled. She lowered her cup in time with the sinking feeling in her stomach. "I don't understand."

Lady Jennie looked over the rim of her cup. "It seems that after you left the salon this morning, the marquess told Henry that to keep you from despoiling the property, or letting some idiot you married do it, he would tie up the estate in court for years, making sure you could not get your hands on it and ruin it for him as well as yourself. I can't for the life of me understand what the man is about. If Henry had the right of it, the man's visit made no sense at all."

As loath as she was to discuss Carson Talmadge further, Rolissa allowed the conversation to go on, and every word of her conversation with the new marquess was repeated and considered. There was much headshaking and expostulating. By the time the subject had been thoroughly combed for hidden meanings, Lady Jennie expressed the feelings of the family with succinctness, even if her words lacked elegance.

"Makes no sense at all. Havey-cavey, if you ask me."

=8=

AFTER TEA, ROLISSA decided that a walk in the park was just the thing to drive away the cobwebs of the drug that had cured her headache. Since Lady Jennie was not fond of walking, and Rolissa had been subjected to more than a sufficiency of Miss Smathers's opinions for the day, it was in the company of her abigail that Rolissa started at a time when many of the fashionable set were leaving the park.

It was Rolissa's intention to ignore most of the course that was considered mandatory for the promenade and merely to stroll about until the fresh air revived her spirits a bit. But she had hardly entered the gates when she was accosted by Mrs. Scruggs, who had been thoughtfully pointed out by an odious gossip as being not only a cit of an oncoming nature but also a cousin of Lady Handing. The intention, obviously, had been to lower the widow in Rolissa's estimation. Rolissa was just turning away to prevent the necessity of meeting the woman when Mrs. Scruggs hastened forward, waving her parasol.

"Yoo-hoo, my dear Lady Rolissa," she called as she came bustling over. "I really must speak to you and tell you what a charming dress that is. I declare, all the modistes must be in quite a taking, falling all over each other for the opportunity to dress you."

Since the garment in question was one Rolissa was partial to, but clearly a style that had been in fashion a year before, and not even one that had caught the fancy of most fashionable females, the compliment was as empty and contrived as Rolissa had expected. Though she was a person sensitive to the feelings of others, blatant toad-eating was something she despised. No hold on her tongue could have prevented her answering. "Thank you, but it is my abigail here who is responsible for dressing me."

"Oh, my dear, what a droll wit," Mrs. Scruggs cooed, but her pinched expression quickened at what she recognised as a cut. The smile that remained was at odds with the sudden narrowing of her eyes.

"It is no wonder all the gentlemen are falling at your feet, and I am persuaded that if the Earl of Ondridge does offer for my cousin, it will only be because you have turned your attentions elsewhere— oh, I should not have told that. I was warned it was only talk within the family. Pray do not repeat it."

Between the pain the information imparted, and the very justifiable anger roused by the woman's deliberate thrust, Rolissa was for a moment speechless, but she quickly recovered. It crossed her mind that she had heard gossip to the effect that, if it were true, Mrs. Scruggs's family would be very much opposed to the match. She took a deep breath and looked the other woman straight in the eye.

"Have no fear, ma'am. *I* am a respecter of family confidences," she said, moving away after wishing the woman a frigid good afternoon.

When Mrs. Scruggs reached out, as if to catch her arm and detain her, Rolissa was thankful that her maid was quick-witted. The abigail moved forward, effectively blocking the cit and directing her attention elsewhere.

"I daresay, there is Miss Elsa Marchlin, my lady, and it looks as if she was desirous of speaking with you."

Rolissa started in the direction indicated, where the tall young lady could be seen strolling with Mr. Jamison. As they approached, Rolissa thought they were certainly a match in looks. Jamie's tall, gangly figure and his habit of walking with his head slightly forward combined with his beaked nose to remind her of nothing so much as a long-legged bird, and the rangy, awkward-looking female with the protruding teeth could have been what nature intended for his mate. Their interest in each other was obvious and unaffected.

When she approached, Rolissa realized the fabrication of her maid's tale, because neither of them had noticed her. They looked up simultaneously, breaking off an absorbed discussion.

"There she is now!" Miss Marchlin announced, and smiled widely at Rolissa, who wondered if they had been discussing her romantic activities. There must be conjecture all over town, she thought, but, then, she doubted if Miss Marchlin, who was certainly no hen-wit, could be led to make such a remark if their conversation had been less than innocent.

"Rolissa, just the one we wanted to see." Jamie nodded. "Would you consider gracing a house party at Ivycroft on your way to Brighton when the season is over? I heard Lady Jennie mention to Tully that you'd be on your way there. Mama is trying to make up her guest list. Lady Jennie has come for the past two years, I think."

"Ivycroft is your family seat?" Rolissa asked.

"Oh, no, the parents take it for the summer. Leased, you know, but one of the spots with the best air, according to my mother. She likes to have a few people in, and snares them on their way to the sea. Usually go to Cornwall myself, but this year I think I will stay closer to London." His smile at Elsa Marchlin made his reasoning clear.

"It sounds delightful, Jamie, but I must leave the final decision to Lady Jennie. For my part, I would love a stay in the country. I think I must be a provincial at heart, but do not, I beg of you, make that public."

Jamie grinned. "If you leave it to your aunt, then I know the answer. The end of the season will see you at Ivycroft."

Rolissa stepped to the side, prepared to bid them good afternoon and continue her walk, but Miss Marchlin reached out, catching her arm. The happy look that had been what Rolissa had first noticed about Elsa had been replaced with concern.

"Won't you walk with us?" she asked. "There are so many things I'd like to know about Northumberland. I do so want to travel about the country. Jamie and I were just speaking about it."

"Yes, do," Jamie seconded her suggestion after meeting the eyes of his companion, but the slight hesitation and his hurried encouragement showed he had been caught off guard and was trying hard to cover it. His eyes, too, showed concern.

Rolissa, remembering Jamie's other efforts to protect her from emotional shocks, thanked them warmly and was determined to refuse. She felt she had no right to let her problems intrude on their time together when they had so little of it. Just then a phaeton pulled to the side of Serpentine Drive, just a few feet away, and Lord Plythford raised his curly brimmed beaver.

"Hallo, Jamie, Elsa. If she'd care for it, could I entice your companion away for a turn about the park?"

Rolissa had intended to refuse, but the glint in Miss Marchlin's eye was enough to give her pause. It was apparent that she was particularly pleased by the turn of events. Though the looks that passed between the two young ladies were purely in a female language, the quick-witted Jamie read them easily and grinned.

"Your maid can trail along with Elsa's," he offered, indicating the soberly dressed woman behind them. "We're heading for the Marble Arch—you'll find us there, Tommy."

When Jamie had handed Rolissa up to her seat in the phaeton, and Plythford had started his cattle, keeping them at a walk, the earl turned and gave her a smile.

"From the look on Jamie's face, I would say we are playing the chess game again."

Rolissa was too fond of Plythford to reply with a fashionable quip. "In a way, though I am unaware of the earlier moves," she said slowly, thinking out what she felt needed to be said. One should not use, without their knowledge, those people who wished you well, she thought.

"I am persuaded you are keeping me from appearing to wear the willow. I am not—or will not. Still, I am vain enough to wish to prevent idle gossip. So injurious to the pride, you see."

"You are not or will not," Plythford said, holding his amusement in check, reading in her hesitation her mental dilemma. "Does that mean your heart is unencumbered, or soon will be? That will be good news for a number of hopeful suitors."

Rolissa lowered her head. "It is goosish of me not to know, but one often misjudges one's feelings." Baring her heart was excruciating. To lighten the conversation, she gave a playful toss of her head. "But I promise, when I have straightened out my thoughts, you will be the first to know."

"Ah, then there may be hope." Plythford smiled and gave the horses the office to trot. "Tremendous hope, because beside me sits not only an heiress, but beauty, wit, and now I find honesty into the bargain. My dear, I am waiting at your feet."

Something in that remark reminded her sharply of her conversation with Ondridge that morning. She laughed with a tinge of bitterness.

"Don't you think, sir, that so much would be an excess when all you're really after is wealth?"

"It *could* be." He affected to consider the question. "If worse came to worse, however, I could find a bird-witted, shrewish antidote for a mistress."

"Fie on you—this is a very improper conversation," Rolissa chided him.

"And that from a young lady who has opted to repeat Lady Jennie's expletives." Plythford looked droll.

Rolissa was laughing as they rounded a turn in the drive and espied the phaeton belonging to Ondridge, stopped just around the bend. Beside the new marquess was Lady Handing. They had been in conversation with Lady Richmond, who was just walking away at that moment, and before Ondridge could put his animals to the trot, Lord Plythford pulled up beside him.

"Hallo, Ondridge. You attending Calver's card party this evening?"

Rolissa nodded at both occupants of the phaeton, noticing the widow's shy acknowledgement and the pink in her cheeks just before she lowered her head and let the wide-brimmed bonnet hide her face from sight.

So he has offered for her, Rolissa thought, and was glad she was at that time grasping the edge of the seat and the handle. Knowing her hands were beginning to tremble, she took care to continue her hold, lest her agitation show, and turned her head as if espying someone across the park, hoping the coolness she felt on her cheeks was not accompanied by the pallor she was afraid might be too apparent. The conversation between the two men continued as she took two deep breaths and deliberately dropped her reticule; in bending forward to retrieve it and its contents from the floor, she was able to regain her composure again.

When she was once more forced to nod to Ondridge as they took their leave, she could see that Lady Handing still had her face averted, but the marquess gave Rolissa a glance of such anger and contempt that she was shocked for a moment, and glad there were no other witnesses to the encounter. Their behaviour would have called forth volumes of gossip and set all the spiteful tongues wagging. No doubt her behaviour had been just as gauche as Lady Handing's, who had, up until this time, impressed Rolissa with her good manners. And Ondridge, with his anger, certainly did not appear the loving swain.

As the carriages separated, it occurred to her that if she did marry Plythford, Carson would have a fight on his hands if he tried to keep her inheritance. It seemed most probable that the gentleman beside her could put up a stronger battle than she would be capable of.

She looked at the handsome Plythford, seriously assessing him for the first time. Tall, broad-shouldered, and with looks that caused people to liken him to a Grecian carving, she could quite frankly admire his striking appearance. Like Tully and Jamie, he was a friend she valued, but not one for whom she had formed a *tendre*. And despite his constant flirting, there was nothing loverlike in his manner toward her.

The satisfaction of giving Ondridge something to worry over was not a lasting emotion. She soon lost her pleasure in the knowledge, and the thought that he had probably offered for Lady Handing depressed her again. She sat, barely acknowledging the people they passed on the ride, and for once she was without Plythford's banter to cheer her. For he, too, was quiet, appearing quite distracted, and drove at a steady pace, only raising his hat to those who greeted him.

Back in Brooke Street, Rolissa found quite enough to keep her mind busy. She had just entered her apartment and had handed her gloves to her abigail when Ollie, her aunt's dresser, cratched at her door and entered without permission.

Rolissa had always heard tales of the top-lofty dressers in London, but Ollie, redoubtable enough when it came to protecting Lady Jennie's interests, was a sweet-faced woman who adored her mistress. When she was not at her duties, she was of a retiring nature. It was clear in her manner that she was very apprehensive.

"I beg your pardon, my lady." She cast a nervous glance at the evening clothes Rolissa's maid was laying out. "Her ladyship has been lying down this last hour, and I fear some illness has overcome her."

"Is it serious?" Rolissa asked, not much alarmed, because while she was concerned for her aunt, she was long ago enured to the exaggerations of her own servants.

"As to that, I could not say, my lady," Ollie replied quietly, her nervous hands at odds with her voice as she pleated her skirt with restless fingers. "It is not in my experience to see her take to her bed needlessly—she has such a contempt for weakness. Miss Smathers was stricken just before my lady and they both seem to be excessively warm."

The lack of an excess of sensibility in Ollie behooved Rolissa to take the dresser's remarks at full value.

"I gather a message has been sent round to the doctor?"

Ollie shook her head. "My lady forbade it, but I think Dr. Adams should be called."

When Rolissa entered her aunt's room, she found her lying on her bed, a cloth over her eyes. Even in the dim light, it was apparent that she was deeply flushed, and her skin was hot.

"Aunt Jennie, you have a good case of influenza," Rolissa said, remembering when the illness had incapacitated half her servants a little more than a year before, and recognising all the symptoms.

Lady Jennie could not have been more outraged if her niece had called her a commoner. "Bosh! It's no such thing! I haven't time for influenza! Do you realize, girl, that one week from today we are to have a ball? The invitations are out, and most of them have been accepted—we've people coming into town especially for it—oooh!" She put her hand up to the cloth, touching it gingerly. "Just give me a little while," she murmured. "I'll be all over it by tomorrow."

Miss Smathers, a person who enjoyed her illnesses to the fullest, was much relieved to learn from the doctor that Rolissa was right in her diagnosis. The thin, elderly woman was making the most of the maids who ran back and forth, warming bricks for her feet, fetching blankets, and trying to coax her into sipping a bit of broth or taking a spoon of restorative pork jelly.

Dr. Adams relieved Rolissa's mind of the worry that either of the ladies was seriously ill. He informed her, with the jocularity that had driven Lady Jennie into a temper, that four or five days would see both invalids on their feet, but to expect them to be fatigued and listless for a while longer. He promised to send a nurse for each and left powders with confusing directions.

Lord Amberly had chosen that particular evening to join a literary crony for dinner, so Rolissa took a tray into the small room that served as the house office. While she nibbled on a slice of ham, she looked about for the plans for the ball. Lying beside the candelabra on the desk was a paisley bound notebook of a convenient size to fit in a lady's reticule. As she took a sip of tea she opened it, idly reading the title page. *Barnstowe Ball, Presenting Lady Rolissa Amberly* had been inscribed in a fine copperplate hand she recognised as Lady Jennie's.

Rolissa nearly choked when she discovered that the rest of the book was completely blank. After the first shock, she decided she had no cause for worry; obviously her aunt and decided some other method would be more convenient for listing her plans. Her search began with considerable confidence, which completely waned as she became hurried and then panicky, but none of the places where her aunt habitually stored her records held any mention of the plans for the ball. Not knowing what else to do, Rolissa sent for Wiggins, the butler, and Mrs. Redgrave, the housekeeper.

When they arrived, they appeared so stiff and disapproving that she hoped she had not taken them from their own meal.

"You are doubtless aware," she began with some temerity, "that we are scheduled to hold a gala ball one week from tonight?"

"Quite aware, my lady," Wiggins answered frostily, making it plain that while Rolissa was approved of by the servants as a guest in the house, she was at the moment overstepping her position.

Rolissa bit her lip. It looked as though her task would be more difficult than she had first suspected. Since she had spoken with the doctor in private, she knew she had one surprise for them. In that she was correct. When informed that Lady Jennie would not be leaving her bed for four and possibly five days, Rolissa thought the look of horror that passed between them was justified. Her efforts at relieving their worries did not shake Wiggins from his attitude that this was house business, and Rolissa, after all, was only a guest. Mrs. Redgrave was a little more open to help.

The housekeeper spoke up weakly, as if all her strength had been drained. "Not one thing has been started, nor has one word of her wishes yet passed my lady's lips."

Wiggins seemed to take exception to what he considered a criticism of his employer and puffed himself up. "Lady Barnstowe is a Singular Person, and has her plans in her head," he said in tones better saved for announcing the regent. "Her talent at organisation is Extraordinary, so a last-minute effort of Hers is quite as efficient as months of planning by some Lesser Hostess."

Rolissa sat back and gazed at the two retainers. Together, with herculean labor, they could still bring about a creditable ball, but without their fullest cooperation any effort on her part would be useless.

"Then possibly I am intruding and neither you nor my aunt needs my assistance at all. Just when is the last minute, Wiggins?"

The butler seemed to waver, but it appeared that common sense was outweighing his pride in the efficiency of the house. "For such a venture, this is it, my lady."

His admission was so grudging she half-expected him to withdraw it at any moment, and with him taking such an attitude, she could not hope for the cooperation the task before them would demand. She had no doubt she could arrange a ball, having run Amberly Manor for years, and a quick eye for what she had seen in London convinced her she could emulate the other hostesses with perhaps just enough originality to keep the affair at Barnstowe House from appearing an exact copy of other balls. But what she needed was a whip to move the Barnstowe servants, who would not willingly take her orders. In the proud countenance of Wiggins, she found her weapon.

"Oh, you poor dears," she murmured, watching the astonishment grow on their faces. "How will we ever contrive, and it is much worse for you. I can retire to Northumberland if we disgrace ourselves, but I am persuaded after years of pride in Barnstowe House and its entertainments, you would be mortified beyond anything and could never face your friends again."

Her words were acting powerfully on Wiggins, who appeared to be seeing a spectre rising from the floor, but she was not finished. "I *could* offer you positions at one of my places in the country, I suppose, but it would not be at all like London. Oh, well, there is no hope for it, we must do our best, and hope we will be able to hold our heads up when it is over. I will be very little help other than authorising expenditure for such things as additional help, and—in London, is it the proper thing to suggest that when the venture is behind us, a gratuity will be presented to each of your underlings whom you recommend as having made a strong effort to ensure its success?"

That question brought about a complete thaw in the rigid attitude of the butler and a ray of hope in the housekeeper. Not only had Rolissa given them a prod with which to urge their underlings on, but she had elevated them to the position of being partly responsible for the promised largesse.

Once she had won their unqualified support, she was nearly overwhelmed with suggestions. Wiggins sent a footman into the yellow salon for the decrepit sewing basket they had often seen by Lady Jennie's side, and it was discovered to be filled with responses to the invitations.

Later that evening, shut away in her room, Rolissa let her mind return to Ondridge, the blushing woman who had been at his side in the phaeton, and the look of anger he had given her when he saw her with Plythford. The pain of the memory brought tears to her eyes, but she resolutely shook them away, opening the weighty volume she had taken from the library. Determined not to think more of the man who must be considered completely out of her life, she immersed herself in *Mrs. White's Guide to Genteel Entertainment.*

During the next few days, there was little time for her to dwell on her heartache. The house was overrun by a host of strange servants. Fortunately, with influenza in the house, it was not considered uncivil for Rolissa to retire from society and refuse morning visits. For the next three days, it seemed that every room was being torn apart. Draperies were taken down, carried out to air and have the dust shaken from their folds. Chandeliers were lowered, and hung like strange skeletons as their lustres were cleaned and polished. Rugs were rolled and relaid. The unused guest chambers were hastily prepared, and every bush in the garden that would support a bedcover was draped as the linens were aired and refreshed by the sun, an expedient that caused Rolissa to slip about the house, trying to escape the indignation of the head gardener and his horde of minions.

Whenever a lull in the activities allowed Rolissa to think about Carson Talmadge, her mind was soon pulled away by some minor catastrophe: The moths had invaded a box of woollen blankets, necessitating the immediate purchase of new ones; a crack had developed in the door of one oven, which threw the confection chef into a tantrum; she must attend the housekeeper on an early morning jaunt to the market to discover which flowers were the most abundant, so they could plan their floral arrangements.

Two days before the ball, the out-of-town guests started arriving, and since the doctor had given orders that Lady Jennie was to remain in bed for an extra day, Rolissa was obliged to provide entertainment for more than a score of complete strangers.

Each night she fell into her bed at an early hour, too tired to linger in her misery, and the ache in her heart was at times outweighed by that in her back and legs, caused by dashing up and down the stair.

When Lady Jennie was allowed out of her room, she walked about the house, listening to the housekeeper, butler, and cooks report on the preparations. She seemed pleased with what Rolissa had accomplished. Her illness, though short and not serious, had left her with little of her accustomed energy, so she was content to leave the arrangements in her niece's hands, only drawing Rolissa's attention to the necessity of hiring men to direct the guests' carriages and prevent what otherwise might be an impossible snarl of vehicles.

When the final night arrived, Rolissa stood at the top of the stair with her aunt, greeting the arrivals. As they had expected, the affair was a tremendous crush, with nearly everyone who had been invited attending, and some bringing unexpected guests.

When she was at last free to enter the ballroom, Rolissa escaped the attentions of the guests as soon as she was able, desiring to step out on the terrace and look down into the garden that had been strung with Chinese lanterns. That was the one part of her preparations she had been forced to plan and execute without being able to see the result before the guests arrived.

"Beautiful," said a voice behind her. She stiffened, hoping to be able to hide the sudden trembling that seemed to overcome her. Her pulse was beating wildly.

"I will tell my aunt you said so," she replied demurely, hoping her voice was steadier to his ears than it was to hers.

"But I understand she has been ill, and the credit for the ball goes to you," Ondridge countered.

"Then I thank you, sir. Now I must return and assist her. As you say, she has not been well." Anxious to leave lest she betray herself, she made as though to brush past him, but he blocked her way.

"Come walk with me in the garden," he said, taking her arm. "After so much effort, I think you deserve the chance to enjoy the beauty you created."

"No, it would not be proper for me to leave everything to Aunt Jennie," she murmured, but even as she objected, she was allowing him to lead her down the stone stair. Every muscle seemed to be following the heart that yearned to be in his company, rather than the head that warned her no good could come of his attentions.

"Are you fatigued?" he asked, as a small sigh escaped her lips. "When I heard that you had taken on the task of arranging this affair, I looked to see you quite overcome by the effort."

"I hope I am not so frail," Rolissa answered.

"You must not be. You are, as I am sure you have been told, at your most ravishing. I particularly like that dress."

Rolissa automatically touched the pale blue crepe, overdraped with silver lace. She was surprised and pleased by the compliment, but at the same time she feared it. Why was he making an effort to be charming? Of all things, that was the last she needed. What she required was time to forget him. She knew she must get away from him.

"I thank you again, but the dress was chosen by Miss Smathers, so to her must go that compliment. Thank you for escorting me while I took the air, but I must return."

"Rolissa, don't go," he said, his voice husky, and he turned, catching both her hands in his. "I want to talk to you."

It was in her mind to say he should be spending his time with his betrothed, but she bit back the words, knowing they would cause her to sound like the jealous female she knew herself to be.

"I doubt we have anything to discuss," she said, her eyes drawn up to his face. She was taken unawares and confused by the look he gave her, his dark eyes a combination of humour and tenderness.

"Rolissa, must we continue to battle?" he murmured softly. The caress in his voice seemed to surround her, shutting out the laughter and the music of the ball, voiding all the pain of the past weeks. Rolissa fought the feeling and controlled herself only with effort. Her tone was bright as she answered him.

"If you wish me to be gay, sir, you must enliven the conversation with a witticism. My days have been filled with the weighty matters of lobster patties and *peu d'amour*, and whether they will be served on silver or crystal."

"Important issues," he agreed, smiling tenderly.

"Oh, vastly," she agreed, trying not to look at him. "Little did I understand, when I made mention of the matter, that this ball is not only one in which my Aunt Jennie was expected to excel, but is a matter of pride to all the servants as well."

"And, of course, you would be one who would care for their pride," he said quietly. Raising first her right hand and then her left, he touched each to his lips. His eyes, never leaving hers, held a gentle expression that seemed to draw her up, bringing her out of herself. She dismissed all the gossip, the fear, the pain, and only knew herself to be with the man she loved.

"One must care for those dependent on them," she said, trying to hold the conversation and give them both a reason for prolonging the glorious moment.

He kissed her fingers again, still smiling down at her. "Then you understand why I'm anxious that we settle the matter of the Letton estates."

She stiffened, at first unable to credit her ears with what she had heard. He had sought her out, made love to her, but only to get her to sign his odious paper. She blushed with shame that she had been so easily taken in. Jerking her hands away, she turned and fled up the path, but after several steps, he caught her arm.

"Let me go—you—you—murderer!" she flung at him.

He released her suddenly and she nearly fell. When she regained her balance, she fled through the garden and up the stair.

═ 9 ═

IT WAS DUE ONLY to years of training in schooling her features that Rolissa was able to return to the ballroom. She was painfully aware that her blush had not receded, but by standing at the back of a group surrounding Lady Jennie, she went for a few minutes unnoticed and had regained much of her composure by the time Tully found her and convinced her to take the floor with him.

She was grateful that he took her lack of sparkle to be fatigue and that she did not have to accept sympathy from him.

"Lovely affair you gave yourself." He grinned. "Too bad you were worked to death before it began."

"Do I show it so much?" She made a moué. "Odious of you to bring it to my attention."

"Then I won't, because others have told you the truth by now, I daresay. May I be so bold as to use Boscomb's term—ravishing?"

She shook her head, thinking not of Boscomb, but of Ondridge when they were in the garden, and how he had made the word sound like a melody—before he had shown his true colours again.

"Hmm." Tully looked down at her, shaking his head. "Then what about—pretty as a shoat, hock deep in mud?"

"You horrid creature!" Rolissa looked up at him with a smile, grateful for his friendship and support. "Just for that, you will consider yourself fortunate if I ever dance with you again—well, perhaps one more time tonight, but you may expect no more than that."

Because of the press of suitors, Rolissa was not to have a second dance with Tully, and she was bereft of both his and Jamie's company for most of the evening. Miss Marchlin, who had postponed her journey home, was drawing most of Jamie's attention. Young Miss

Singer was bringing a sparkle to Tully's eye, and her prudent aunt had obviously judged it proper to allow him slightly more time in the young lady's company.

Rolissa was even missing the witticisms of Lord Plythford, though she knew he had arrived while she was in the receiving line, and had even requested the honour of taking her in to supper. She looked around and was just in time to see him as he entered from the terrace in the company of Ondridge. More surprising was the look of accord between them as they traded a few words and parted just inside the door. After the glances of anger and contempt that she had received from Ondridge just for being in the company of the man he had called a rogue, she had expected Plythford to be the last person the earl would hold in esteem.

But why not? she thought. The only difference between the two is that Plythford is aboveboard in *his* dealings.

Trying to hold that thought, she stifled the tears as Ondridge, across the room, led Lady Handing out onto the floor. Altogether, it seemed to Rolissa that she was living through the longest and most miserable evening of her life.

Fortunately for Rolissa, there was only a week left of the official season, and then they would be on their way to Ivycroft. She was looking forward to a rest, not only from the rigours of the season, but from having to guard against her emotions every time she encountered Ondridge. He was still constantly in the company of the widow, although the last time Rolissa had walked in the park, she noticed that Mrs. Scruggs had hastily taken another path. Rolissa had no doubt it was because, for all the woman's boasting remarks, there had been neither an official announcement of a betrothal nor a notice in the *Gazette*.

Finally the last ball closed the season, Lady Jennie created havoc among the servants as sundry items of furnishings were suddenly discovered to be indispensable to their comfort in Brighton, and the trip was begun. At the last minute, and much to the surprise of the ladies, Lord Amberly decided to accompany the household to the sea, which called for some minor rearranging. But at last Lady Jennie's carriage, carrying herself and Rolissa, Miss Smathers, and Henry, set forward leading a string of equipage that would have done credit to the regent.

Lady Jennie had been adamant about the hour at which they must leave London, timing the entire journey so they arrived for luncheon at the Leaping Hart Inn. The ancient hostel was known for its food and was a favourite spot with the fashionable set who travelled the road to and from Brighton each year. When they arrived in the courtyard, nearly a score of private carriages was in sight, and beneath the shade of several large trees, trestle tables had been erected, where coachmen, grooms, and quite a number of lady's maids were being served.

As he stepped down from the coach, Lord Amberly looked askance at all the bustle. "Did we think to bespeak a private parlour?" he asked worriedly.

Lady Jennie gave him a look of disdain. "No more than I would at Ivycroft," was her terse reply.

As they entered they were met by a robust man, obviously their host, who led the way down a passage and showed them into what appeared to be a common room with several long, rough-hewn tables, surrounded by sturdy ancient chairs that had been worn to a glassy smoothness by time and use. Not aware of the existence of the Leaping Hart until that day, Rolissa had no idea of its fame, and was surprised to find all the large number of occupants at least familiar to her—all members of the *ton* whom she had known or seen in London. As they were crossing the room she spied Miss Singer, who smiled shyly. Lady Jennie had also seen the young lady, and turned to Rolissa.

"Go and sit with her—be more pleasant than joining Lady Rusale, which I suppose I am obliged to do."

While Lady Jennie crossed the room to the dowager who was her prime rival in both eccentricity and a bold tongue, Rolissa joined Miss Singer, who was accompanied by her younger sister Jane and her aunt, Mrs. Lindstrom. Jane was hardly more than fifteen and would never be her sister's equal in beauty, but neither did she have her sister's shy character. Their aunt was what the young gentlemen called a dragon—a shrewd, watchful chaperone. This particular one was known for her bitter gossip.

"You're on your way to Ivycroft?" Miss Singer asked as Rolissa was seated.

"Just as speedily as we can go. You cannot imagine how glad I am to be out of London."

"Oh, but I can," Miss Singer replied with feeling. "I am never comfortable at those great balls. I prefer smaller entertainments, and smaller towns."

Just then a waiter brought a tray of food. He was followed by a second and a third server, and they were busy with their meal. Though she had little appetite, Rolissa found herself succumbing to the tantalising aroma of an excellent game pie, which was followed by a brace of ducks, loin of venison, broccoli spears, and a gooseberry tart. After their morning journey, both the other young ladies were engaged in doing full justice to the meal, and most of the conversation was carried on by their aunt.

". . . but I will never understand Rachel's dislike of London," she was saying. "With all the interesting things going on and everyone talking about—"

"I think the London gossip is terrible," Miss Singer interrupted, giving her aunt a quelling stare. That silenced Mrs. Lindstrom for the moment, but shortly afterward a large party entered and three young ladies hardly past schoolroom age waved frantically to the Singer girls. Mrs. Lindstrom eyed them warily and motioned Jane to get to her feet.

"You and Rachel go over and speak to them," she said imperiously. "I declare, I will not have them and their nonstop tongues over here."

Rolissa kept to herself the thought that the odious Mrs. Lindstrom could not abide any gossip but her own.

Obediently, the Misses Singer excused themselves and went over to greet their friends while Mrs. Lindstrom chattered away at Rolissa about who said what at the last ball. Then she leaned forward confidentially.

"I must tell you what Rachel is so goosish as to think you would not want to hear." She cast a glance at her nieces, who were deep in conversation with their friends, and then gave Rolissa a conspiratorial smile. "You were so right to give that horrid Ondridge the air. A man of most infamous intentions, in my opinion."

Rolissa was neither interested in Mrs. Lindstrom's opinion, nor desirous of discussing the new Marquess of Letton with her, but before she could say so, the woman started again.

"My younger brother is a cleric at St. Paul's, and would you believe—the man bought a special license, and by use of his wily tongue, he's convinced the bishop not to fill in the names. Can you imagine! Talk about an opportunist! I suppose he will drag that poor Lady Handing to the altar, or, if not, catch anyone he can reach with a fortune large enough to interest him. I am convinced, there is nothing that man will not do."

Rolissa had been pushing the rest of a gooseberry tart around on her plate, trying to concentrate on it and block what Mrs. Lindstrom was saying. Wondering if the trouble she was having in breathing was caused by the oppressive heat or by the news she had just received, she prayed she could bear up under the strain and not faint. If she did, doubtless that, too, would become grist for the woman's cutting tongue.

"My dear, you are so fortunate to be free of him," Mrs. Lindstrom cooed. "You were wiser than the rest."

Rolissa was hard-pressed to find an answer. Had her mind obeyed her, she knew she would have been betrayed by the trembling in her throat, but at that moment the Misses Singer returned to the table, immediately followed by Lady Jennie, Miss Smathers, and Lord Amberly.

Lady Jennie greeted Mrs. Lindstrom. "Shall we see you presently at Ivycroft? Perhaps we can get up a game of whist tonight."

"If I have not taken to my bed from the effects of this terrible heat and all the chatter," Mrs. Lindstrom replied, giving her nieces a significant glance. "Jane is so excited she has almost driven me into a migraine."

"Then why not exchange places with my niece?" Lady Jennie suggested. "Although there is nothing we can do about the weather, the young ladies could ride in one coach and allow their youthful spirits full rein."

At once the idea was acclaimed by Jane, and Miss Singer gave a quieter endorsement as well. Rolissa, who had had more than enough of Miss Smathers's opinions about Ondridge, was agreeable as long as she did not have to endure the company of Mrs. Lindstrom. When they started the shorter leg of their journey to Ivycroft, the carriage with the three young ladies was in line and only a short distance behind that of Lady Jennie. The day had indeed turned unseasonably warm, even for high summer, and the three girls were busy with fluttering fans, trying to alleviate the stifling atmosphere inside the coach.

Rolissa soon found that Mrs. Lindstrom had not been exaggerating in her summation of Jane's chatter. Once away from the older members of the party, the girl rattled nonstop, and much of her conversation centered around Lord Tulane. It was obvious that she thought her sister would be making the catch of the season if she could secure the handsome viscount for a husband. So extravagant were her comments on him that only the absence of any sign of jealousy prevented Rolissa from deciding the younger girl might have a schoolgirl crush on Tully. Miss Singer was blushing furiously and trying in vain to stop her sister's talk.

Then the subject, aided by Miss Singer, veered to the house party. Rolissa, hungry for quiet rides and walks about the peaceful countryside rather than games of whist and picnics, was not much interested until Jane jerked her out of her reverie.

". . . and with Mr. Jamison, who is spending a week there before going on to Marchlin Hall"—she raised her eyebrows, showing she knew about the unannounced engagement of Jamie and Elsa Marchlin—"there will be Viscount Tulane, the Marquess of Letton, Lord Plythford, and—"

Rolissa swung on Miss Singer. "Is Carson Talmadge also going to Ivycroft?"

"Lord Tulane said he was," Miss Singer replied, not meeting Rolissa's eyes.

"Well, I for one do not understand why he should be," Jane announced. "It seems to me, if he has really bought a special license, then he should be going somewhere to be married. Who would want a wedding down here? When Rachel marries the viscount, it will be in London, in St. Paul's, and—"

"Jane! You will not say such things!" Rachel Singer cried. She turned imploringly to Rolissa, her cheeks flaming. "Pay her no heed—she's not yet out of the schoolroom and has no idea of the harm she could cause. I pray you will not let the viscount know she talks so. He has not"—she frowned at her sister—"he has not tried to fix his attentions with me, and would be sorely put out if he were to learn what you are saying."

That thought seemed to strike the younger girl forcibly, because she paled and bit her lip, staring through the window. Rolissa doubted that the sister's enthusiasm for the match would find disfavour with Tully, since he had made no secret of the direction of his interest.

It was not to be expected that a young, lively girl like Miss Jane Singer could long contain her tongue, but when she spoke again, it was on what she thought to be a safer topic: Carson Talmadge.

"Well, I still think it shabby to expect someone to marry you and take them off to a place like this to do it," she reiterated.

"I wish you will cease to speak of that, too," Miss Singer said. She fanned herself with the speed of agitation and cast an apprehensive glance toward Rolissa, but her sister, observing it and correctly reading her fears, waved them aside.

"Oh, everyone knows he tried to fix his interest with Lady Rolissa, but she was too smart to be taken in." Jane smiled on Rolissa, leaving no doubt she thought herself in the company of a female of particular perspicacity, and feeling very pleased about it.

Rolissa, despite her emotions of a week before, could no longer sit still and hear Carson Talmadge so maligned. "It is not necessary for him to dangle after a fortune," she said quietly. "I have reason to know he inherited a great deal of wealth, both from his brother and from the late marquess."

Jane nodded wisely, as only a young and very spirited girl could. "But you know what my aunt says—the greatest danger of ill-gotten gains is that they create an insatiable appetite for more. And if they were come by honestly, why does he keep that criminal as a tiger, is what my aunt wants to know."

"Jane, do not repeat that slanderous gossip—"

"It is only slanderous if it is untrue," Jane argued back. "And if there is truth to it, Lady Rolissa should know, because maybe he will use that awful man to help him take her away and make her marry him—"

"My dear—" Rolissa broke in, irritated beyond being able to hold her tongue, but Miss Singer was before her and sharper.

"You will stop it this instant! I know you only repeat what you hear, but it is not at all respectable, especially when coming from the mouth of a schoolroom miss!"

Jane looked so downcast that Rolissa was moved, in spite of her anger, to try to smooth things over a bit.

"Jane, the marquess could not be only interested in a rich wife. He is apparently trying to fix his interest with Lady Handing, and while she may command the first style of excellence, she is not overly wealthy."

Jane appeared to be grateful for Rolissa's consideration, and launched into yet another *on dit,* much to the dismay of her benefactress.

"My aunt says, and I think she's right, that you should take care. He may not get Lady Handing."

"Jane!" Miss Singer was outraged, but there was no stopping her sister.

"I heard the cit side of her family wants her money, and they don't want her anywhere near the marquess unless they can watch what goes forward, and, of course, the Jamisons are not inviting cits to Ivycroft. I think it is odious of her relatives to push themselves like that. Lady Handing is a very nice person." This last observation was spoken in a very different voice and showed a different, kinder nature behind that of the odious little gossip-monger. Unfortunately, the child had made her aunt her model. But beneath the gossip was at least some of the sweetness of her older sister.

While Rolissa was looking more kindly upon the girl sitting across from her, the coach slowed and turned to the left, travelling through a pair of open gates and up an avenue lined with ancient trees. The air seemed close and tight, and Rolissa leaned closer to the window, hoping to catch a whiff of the breeze that was gaining strength by the moment. As she looked out she noticed a building on which extensive repairs were being made.

"Everywhere there seem to be improvements," she commented, thinking of those she had seen at Luthforth.

Miss Singer leaned forward to look and nodded calmly. "Lord Tulane told me it was the same on all the properties the marquess inherited from his brother. He is forever bringing things back to order."

Just then there came a flash of lightning and a roll of thunder, but though both Misses Singer jumped away from the windows, Rolissa was too much struck by the comment to notice.

"Does Ivycroft belong to Carson Talmadge?" she asked, suddenly feeling a weakness go through her.

Naturally it was Jane who answered. "Not only Ivycroft, but almost everything else around here when one adds in the second inheritance. He's like a king in this part of the country. My aunt says he can do anything he likes, commit—my, the wind is getting strong." The sudden change of subject was accompanied by a wary look in her sister's direction.

Rolissa sank back on the cushions, staring through the window at the trees that were twisting in the rising wind. The impending storm blended together with the gossip to fill her with renewed doubts and an entirely new fear. She tried to shake them away, but in their place came the conversation she had heard through the window at the Richmond ball.

This is nothing but foolishness, she told herself. The memory of his lovemaking in the garden the night of her ball came back as clearly as if it were taking place again. If he was willing to make love to her, would he be willing to marry her for her double inheritance? He hadn't showed any objection when only the Amberly fortune was at stake, and had been on the verge of offering for her until she stopped him. He had shown every evidence of wanting the complete Letton estate intact.

Nonsense. He knows I will not have him and he could not possibly force me. But could he? She could not believe it.

More likely, the names had been left off the license he had obtained because of Lady Handing's relatives. Ondridge was doubtless miles away, heading for some secret rendezvous where he would meet the little widow, and they would escape to a parsonage and be married quietly. There was nothing for Rolissa to fear.

There was no hope left, either.

The wind had become stronger when the coach pulled up in front of the huge, spreading manor house. Rolissa sat and waited, hoping to compose herself, while the footmen assisted the other young ladies from the vehicle. Then she moved close to the door and put one hand on her hat. A hand was held out to her. As she left the shelter of the vehicle, the wind caught her hat and she was forced to keep a close hold on it. One foot was on the bottom step and she was groping for the ground with the other as she blinked her eyes against the windblown dust. She turned her head, trying to avoid the grit, and froze. She was staring into the rodentlike face of Soames, Ondridge's tiger, and he in turn was eyeing her with an expression of intense pleasure on his evil-looking countenance.

Suddenly, every fear came rushing back and she jerked away from him. Trying to keep her balance against the wind, she staggered backward and collided with the wheeler of the coach, which started to rear and fight its traces.

With a shout, Soames started toward her. With Jane's speculations ringing in her ears, she abandoned all common sense in her panic, turned, and rushed toward the vehicle that belonged to her aunt, not even noticing that Soames had stopped by the frightened horse and was trying to calm it. Already nervous from the sudden high wind and lightning, the rest of the team had started to plunge and a postillion from the other team rushed back to help, leaving only one man standing with a slack hand on the bridle of the leaders harnessed to Lady Jennie's coach.

That team, too, was restless with the storm and the noise behind them, but Rolissa ran up close to the left wheeler, hoping to see the familiar coachman. What tale she would tell him, she had no idea, but there was no need for fabrication. He was not on the seat.

That she had never driven a team did not occur to Rolissa. In a panic that had its seeds in her childhood, and had been brought to fruit by the gossip of London and Jane's chatter, she only knew she had to escape. With a nimbleness that came from her schooldays in Northumberland, she was on the seat, the reins and the whip in her hand.

The whip struck the back of the leader at the same moment a bolt of lightning cracked overhead, and that was enough for the restive horses. As they lunged forward, Rolissa was dimly aware of the startled post boy, but she was unable to understand his shouts as the coach rolled by, circling the drive, picking up speed as she bowled down the avenue.

Once the coach was fully in motion, Rolissa forgot all her fears of Ondridge. She was too occupied in trying to remain on the seat, its leather worn smooth by years of contact with drivers' wool-clad bottoms. Although a man's feet would have reached the floor of the box to brace him, Rolissa's shorter limbs could not. Unable to steady herself except with her hands, she had no leverage to draw back the ribbons, and the job horses that had been hired at the last changing station were tough-mouthed animals. With no tug to check them, and the wind and the lightning making their fear as great as Rolissa's, they charged down the avenue too fast to make the turn into the public road.

Fortunately for the moment, a country track intersected the public way just across from the entrance to Ivycroft, and they galloped across, racing along the rutted lane as it twisted and turned.

Dropping the whip, Rolissa reached behind her, clutching the rail at the back of the seat, barely staying in place. She desperately hoped there would be someone on the track who could slow or stop the team, but the area seemed like a wilderness, and with only one hand holding the reins, she was unable to prevent the horses from turning to the right or the left as other, more likely tracks came available.

Hope flared as she espied ahead what she thought was a habitation, but as they drew closer, she saw it was a ruin with roofless stone walls. As they passed nearly a quarter of a mile away, she gave up hope and turned her eyes ahead, searching for someone who would be able to lend her aid.

Hope rose and died as she saw another structure, but although twilight had deepened, and night was coming on, no lights showed the house was occupied. She gave it a wistful glance as the vehicle careened around a curve and it was lost to sight. But then she had no other thought for it, because ahead, directly in the middle of the road, a cow stood gazing calmly at the runaway team bearing down on it.

Rolissa screamed, thinking their wild ride would end in the death of the cow, the horses, and likely herself, but the terrified team swerved to the right, swinging the wildly swaying coach into the shallow ditch with no lessening of speed. The jolt threw Rolissa into the air, and she landed on the edge of a field mercifully bordered with a thick hedge, overgrown with vines.

Her landing was still a severe blow, and she lay, half in and half out of the mass of vines, stunned and knocked breathless by her fall. When she tried to move, she found herself impeded by the vines and had to disentangle herself from the clinging tendrils, but she discovered that only her right arm, where her shawl had left it bare, had been scratched. Mercifully, nothing seemed to be broken or wrenched.

The coach and team were out of sight on the winding track, and as she sat, trying to get her breath, the cow, with a total disregard for the accident she had caused, went ambling along in the direction of the team and the coach.

Rolissa looked up at the sky. The wind was still blowing fiercely, and the lightning was casting an eerie glow on the evening. She started to walk down the lane in the direction she had come, hoping to find shelter.

The only place she had seen that would offer protection from the wind and possibly the rain to follow was the dark house, the second place she had passed.

= 10 =

ROLISSA CONTINUED DOWN the track until she saw the house again, whereupon her resolve to shelter there was shaken by its abandoned appearance. The overgrown state of the grounds and heavy shutters that covered the windows leaped into startling relief in the intermittent flashing of the lightning. It was so like something out of a ghost tale that she shuddered at the thought of nearing it. Still, if rain was to follow the lightning, she would be in desperate need of shelter.

She steeled herself against her disinclination and turned toward the house. Until that time, the primary obstacle to her progress had been the wind, but as she changed direction, it became an unwanted ally. Like some unseen force pushing her on to her fate, it caught at her skirts, pummelled against her back, and lengthened her stride. When she reached the door, she grasped the latch, pushing her weight against the ancient scarred wood, aided by the strength of the wind. As the door gave easily under her hand, she was propelled forward and fell headlong into the entrance hall.

For the second time that evening, she lay stunned and breathless. Dimly, she heard a male voice give out with a startled oath, and there were hurried footsteps in her direction. The wind stopped buffeting her as the door was closed. She was just struggling to rise when strong hands aided her to stand, and she looked up into the surprised and frowning face of Carson Talmadge.

"What—" he muttered. "Here, come to this chair. You look as if you've been in a war. Are you injured—hurt—?"

Too worn to struggle, she allowed him to lead her to a chair and sat staring at him as he took a seat on the small footstool close by. Though he gazed back at her with an amazement no less than her own, he allowed her time to collect her wits, neither questioning her presence nor explaining his. For some moments they sat in silence. Then the extent of her folly came home to Rolissa.

What have I done? she asked herself. She would have been safer at Ivycroft. In running away, she had thrown herself into the very danger she had feared. She gazed at him, still in silence, wondering how she might escape, and questioning at the same time the surprise, anger, and concern that flickered across his countenance.

Slowly, an awareness of her surroundings grew on Rolissa. She noticed that the room was comfortably furnished and clean, a contrast to the abandoned appearance of the exterior and grounds. There was an incongruity about Carson Talmadge, also. He was dressed in the approved style of the country gentleman, with buckskin breeches and top boots, but his elegantly cut coat was wrinkled and soiled, while his cravat was crushed. One end of the mathematical had loosened and protruded above his collar, a condition he absently corrected as he returned her gaze. His waistcoat was unbuttoned, and his hair, normally brushed into the first style of fashion, was all awry.

The first thought that came to Rolissa was that to allow himself to reach such a dishevelled state he was most likely in his cups, and she wondered what secret and illicit circumstance she had happened upon. Immediately, an event of an unexpected nature gave her thoughts quite a different turn.

"Giddup, hossy!" a child squealed, and from a doorway behind her dashed two tiny individuals, approximately two years in age. They were, she realised, twins, dressed in neatly pressed and pleated nightshirts and wearing small blue felt slippers, though only one had slippers on both feet. The other little fellow, stumbling over the corner of the faded carpet, had lost a shoe, and he stopped to pick it up, rushing to Ondridge, putting the offending article in his hand.

As they accosted Ondridge, they grabbed his legs, jumped up and down, clutched his well-cut coat, and scrambled up on his thighs, each using one of his muscular legs for a mount. Rolissa watched, fascinated, as he suffered this assault upon his person, giving the children only enough attention to prevent one from tumbling off and falling to the floor.

In keeping with her first thought about him and the house, she began to fear she had discovered some secret hideaway where he kept his illegitimate offspring, but as his hands encircled the boys' small waists in an almost unconscious gesture of protection, the look on his face was not one of a man trying to hide or protect a folly. There was about his manner an aura of urgency that suddenly interpreted for Rolissa the meaning of what she observed. Her mouth opened in wonder.

"Whippy's sons!" she whispered, too astonished to speak aloud. "You have been hiding them!"

Ondridge shifted as if coming out of some far distant thought. He glanced down at the blond, curly haired boys who were holding tightly to his arms as he bounced his heels on the carpet.

"That must remain our secret," he said quietly. "Their lives may depend on the fact that everyone thinks they were in that carriage."

"But how—why—?" Before Rolissa could overcome her confusion and ask her questions, the opening of a door caused her to look over her shoulder, and so she observed the approach of a small, plump woman with grey hair, bright eyes, and a sweet expression. Upon seeing Rolissa, she paused, gave the younger woman a comprehensive look, and rushed forward, her sympathy instantly engaged.

"My poor dear, have you been in an accident?" When she had been assured by Rolissa that she had not sustained any injury, the woman insisted on taking the lady to her own room, explaining apologetically that most of the rooms in the house were closed.

Under the motherly attitude of Miss Holcomb, the children's nurse, Rolissa allowed herself to feel the drain the evening's experiences had made on her strength. She gratefully accepted the woman's attentions, and drank the tea that was brought to her. It was from the nurse, upon whom the knowledge that the young lady was a relative of the twins acted powerfully, that Rolissa heard the story of how they had disappeared.

"May the Lord forgive me if I have done wrong, my lady, but I do not think I have," the woman told her. "I was that terrified, I had no idea what to do, you see. That awful morning, I had my little gentlemen at the back of the garden, letting them run and have a nice bit of shout and squeal, you know. Then there was the Earl of Ondridge, his face as pale as his neckcloth. He was just tying his horses up, there being no way of reaching the stable or the house from that back lane. He had started through the gate when he saw the boys, and I will allow he suddenly went even paler, as if he had seen a ghost, or as I later learned, the vision of another disaster in the making."

She shook her head as she relived the memory. "Then everything was like a nightmare. He grabbed up my little fellows, saying something about they were going to be murdered, and all I could do was run along behind him, trying the best I could to get my babies back. The next thing I knew we were in that racing thing of his, and he was driving like a madman, and I was so busy trying to keep my little lords from tumbling out I had not even the strength to set up a screech, not that there would have been anyone to hear me.

"We were almost here before he slowed and told me about the poor marquess, and how someone seemed to be trying to do away with all the family, he thought. By that time, I was beginning to credit some of the stories I had heard about him, though I will tell you they were never believed at Letton Manor. I was trying to come up with a scheme for getting my little gentlemen to safety, but bless me, if the earl didn't bring the vicar and his wife that very day, so I would feel easier, knowing someone I trusted knew where we were. It was to keep me from getting some hen-witted idea of running away, he told me right to my head, but I didn't mind that, you may be sure."

"Are you here alone?" Rolissa asked, thinking one small woman was no protection for the children if the secret became known.

"Bless me, no." Miss Holcomb smiled. "The earl brought me two maids, a cook, and two grooms that sleep in the house and have big nasty pistols, but we go to bed at night feeling safe."

"And he comes to visit the children," Rolissa mused aloud.

"That he does." The nurse chuckled complacently. "And with such frolicking play that when he takes himself off, it is all we can do to handle them—you have no idea. It will take the devil's own to control them once he has them into his own house—you know he is their guardian—or says the will appointed him."

"They are to live with him?"

"So he says, just as soon as there is proof enough to stop that murdering rascal."

The warmth that had invaded Rolissa when she heard of the earl's care of the children dissolved with the reminder that there was someone unknown killing off various members of the family.

"Do you know who killed the Marquess of Letton?"

Miss Holcomb's face puckered as she shook her head. "I think the earl has some suspicions, but he refused to tell me. He says, because of my little lords, it is better that I suspect and fear everyone."

Their conversation was interrupted by a knock at the door. An elderly maid stepped in and announced that the children were nodding and ready for their beds, and that the covers were being laid in the dining room for my lord and lady's dinner.

When Rolissa entered the drawing room, she smiled at the sight of Ondridge walking around the room with a sleepy toddler in each arm. Their soft golden curls were gleaming brightly against his dark coat as their heads lay on his shoulders. One little fellow shifted and a sleepy voice said, "Giddup," whereupon the lord pranced gently until the small head fell back on his shoulder again.

"Enough!" whispered Miss Holcomb. "They will be demanding a horsey ride every night before sleep." She reached out to take one of the boys, but Ondridge stepped back.

"I'll take them up," he said with a smile, and preceded the nurse from the room.

Rolissa followed the maid into the dining room and wandered about for some minutes, though the passage of time went unnoticed. She felt as if her mind had been run through a butter churn. All her doubts about Ondridge had been swept out; guilt that she had suspected him of wrongdoing was making itself felt, along with numerous questions that followed one another as if linked in a chain.

She was shortly joined by the earl, who had tidied his clothing and looked hardly the worse for his games with the twins. When she tried to speak about her feelings, Ondridge insisted that first they have their dinner in peace. They could talk later.

Their meal was one of cottage simplicity, consisting only of ham with fresh asparagus, newly baked bread, and blancmange for dessert. The household was clearly geared to care for the children rather than guests, and Ondridge seemed to expect no more than he was given. To Rolissa's surprise, she was hungry and did full justice to the meal set before her. By the time the covers were removed, she had any number of questions, but there was one thought foremost in her mind, and it had to be aired first. With a shyness uncommon in her, she gazed at Ondridge.

"I am persuaded there are not enough words to express my apology," she said slowly. "What I said to you—the things I thought—"

There was a tightening around his mouth, but the hand that waved away her apology was negligent. "Why should you be any different than the rest?" His lips curved in a sneer. "At least you had both the courage and the honesty to say it to my face."

"I am so sorry," Rolissa went on, feeling she must say what was in her mind. "I refused to believe it at first—I think it was the title and your insistence on managing the Letton properties that caused me to change my mind, and I understand that less now than I did then. If you knew the children were alive, then you knew it was not yours. Why did you claim it?"

His look was at first scornful, and then with a sigh he softened his expression, as if he could not hold her to blame for misinterpreting his actions. He leaned forward, his elbows on the edge of the table, supporting his hands and resting his chin on them.

"To convince everyone I believed the boys had been killed with Whippy. That was murder, you know, and cleverly done."

"How can you be sure?" Rolissa asked, because even with all the talk, no one had been able to say for sure that the loss of the carriage wheel had been more than an accident.

"I was on my way to see Whippy, and I came on the carriage not long after the accident. The horses were still plunging, but the axle was trapped where the track had been gouged to create a hold and throw undue strain on a badly set wheel. The next day it rained. The cut in the track now looks as if it were made by the rain washing away the soil, but I could see then it was cut out by pick and spade."

"But wouldn't the killer have been somewhere around, to make sure his plan worked?" Rolissa asked. "Wouldn't he know whether or not the boys were in the carriage?"

"I doubt it," Ondridge replied. "He is too sly to risk it. More reason for me to use the title. Even if he knows the little blighters are alive, he won't expect me to be hiding them."

"But that makes you look to be the guilty party," Rolissa objected. "How can you expect people to search for the truth when *you* are the one who is giving them every reason to suspect you? You're throwing dust in their eyes."

Ondridge gave her a level look. "The villain may get careless if he thinks he is safe. I'm less concerned with public opinion than you are. I am hoping the one who is responsible will come after me next. If he truly believes the twins are dead, then I have to be at the top of his list." His jaw was as tight as the fist he clenched. "He will find *me* ready for him."

"Yes, but why would you be next?" Rolissa asked, her eyes widening as she thought of the obvious answer. "It all concentrated on you, all the titles, the entailed property and much of the wealth, and who would benefit except—but that means you think it is *Tully!*" She stared unbelieving as he twirled his wineglass between his fingers.

The silence became oppressive as she sat looking around the room, back at the earl, and down at the damask cloth on the table. His restraint was enough for her to know he agreed, but she was unable to accept the only plausible answer.

"Not Tully," she said, shaking her head miserably.

"Then who else could it be? Who else benefits after me?" Ondridge looked at her calmly as he pushed his glass away and stood up. "Well, the storm has passed. We had better gt you back to Ivycroft. They'll have searchers out, and I don't want them looking here."

It was a measure of Rolissa's inner turmoil that she had not been aware of the storm, and had forgotten her precipitous departure from Ivycroft. She felt a stab of guilt as she thought of Miss Smathers, who was doubtless suffering hysterics, and of the concern that both Lady Jennie and Lord Amberly would be feeling.

While they stood in the hall, waiting for the earl's horse to be brought around, Rolissa's talent for thinking of details brought another question to mind.

"How will you explain the disappearance of the nurse and the twins when—you take them to your house?" She had hesitated, not yet able to say, "When you have proved Tully a murderer."

"We won't. They'll show up in the village, the nurse will claim to have just recovered her memory, and she will have no idea where she has been or how they managed since the wreck, so no one can fasten on some detail and prove her wrong. I will see that she is given credit for having cared for the little tykes during a trying time. She will be a heroine."

"Then you are going to hold to the story that they were in the carriage?"

"The problems will be lessened if the story does not become too complicated," he replied.

"Then I trust you have seen to it that the clothing they were wearing will show that it has been worn through weeks or months of living in a cave or some such. And what happens if this condition lasts long enough so they have grown out of what they had on that morning? You cannot have them reappear in their pleated night frocks."

"No, by God!" Ondridge looked much struck by that idea.

As they left the old house, Ondridge put his hand on her arm and she recalled the last time he had done so, when he led her into the garden on the night of the Barnstowe ball. She remembered, too, his object at the time.

"Now I know why you were so anxious to have control of the Letton properties," she said. "They are not mine at all, but why did you not tell me the truth? I would have gladly cooperated if I had understood."

"I dared not risk it," he replied. "I willingly trust no one with the secret. I take you into my confidence now because you stumbled on the truth, and no matter what society thinks, I seldom go about strangling women and children. I have to trust you will not allow a desire to be the first with gossip to endanger the lives of those little characters."

Rolissa was stung to learn he thought she might be callous or unthinking enough to let their secret out. "I assure you, sir, I will not betray them. Nor would you have found their fortune wasted if I had not discovered the secret for myself."

"That is something I could not count upon," Ondridge replied with equal reserve. "From what I've seen of your suitors, you were very likely to choose a man who would have dissipated both your inheritances in a very short time."

"And you think me such a goose that I would accept one of them?" She glared up at him, wondering why they could not have a conversation of any length before they were at daggers drawn, but his insults were not to be borne.

"I am not responsible for who addressed me at a social engagement, but save you and Plythford, I am not regularly seen in the company of gazetted fortune hunters. The Earl of Plythford, as you probably know, is a companion rather than a romantic interest."

"But could I have been certain of that?" Suddenly, his voice was gentle, and as if a heavy curtain had dropped, exposing him as he stood, his eyes touched her with a hunger that left her shaken. His hand gently held her arm. His strong resonant voice trembled slightly.

"Beauty and charm such as yours can command far more than fortune hunters, of that I am aware—but with so much loveliness, and your wealth, too, at stake, how could I be sure you were not to be taken in by the unscrupulous? I have no doubt that you are in danger from the hearts of many men—" He stopped speaking and turned away abruptly, as if noticing the horse for the first time.

Rolissa, her heart soaring with the thrill of the desire she had seen in his eyes, tried to make light of the situation.

"They say in town that I am in much more danger from you." She wanted to add the danger came from her own heart, and was on the brink of admitting it, no matter that it was unthinkably forward, but he stopped her with a sudden reply.

"And that, ma'am, is a danger nonexistent," he said with frost on his voice. "You are in no danger that I am any longer seeking to fix your attention on anything but this horse."

Rolissa was glad, at that moment, to be busy with mounting the block and taking her place behind the saddle. She was thankful, too, of the darkness that hid what must show on her face. Had she suffered all the pain of her doubts, and then had them resolved, only to find he would never fill the place in her life that corresponded with the one in her heart? She blinked back the tears, determined not to allow him to know of her true feelings. He would doubtless make a match of it with Lady Handing, whose serenity would never lead him into the contretemps that often occasioned between him and Rolissa. The widow would be a wonderful second mother to the twins, she was sure, but the thought gave her no pleasure at all.

They rode slowly along the dark, rutted track, and Rolissa, positioned on the horse's rump as if Ondridge had in truth found and rescued her from a long, uncomfortable walk, kept her arms around his waist to retain her seat. Her position was at the same time both a joy and a torture. To be in such proximity, to be totally aware of his strong muscular body as he rode easily in the saddle, was a delight that would be over all too quickly. To have the awareness of the shelter and protection offered by his strong back and wide shoulders was a pleasure she would remember all her life—remember with longing and regret.

All too quickly, they reached Ivycroft. Ondridge led Rolissa inside, and she was immediately accosted by Miss Smathers.

"Oh, my dearest." The little woman flung herself on Rolissa, her tears flowing. It was Lady Jennie who, after being reassured that her niece was only tired and not injured, sent her to her room in the company of her maid and would have no more ado.

As she was led up the steps, Rolissa heard Ondridge telling the assembled guests how, when she had seen the horses ready to bolt, she had climbed onto the coachman's seat, hoping to hold them. When she turned the corner of the hallway, he was agreeing with Jamie that while her action was foolhardy, she had been brave in the extreme. Rolissa was glad he had the foresight to have a plausible explanation at hand.

Tired as she was, she lay staring into the darkness after her maid bade her a reluctant good night. There was no hiding the relief in her heart that Ondridge was truly innocent of the rumours, but stabbing like a knife was the information that he no longer had the desire to fix any interest with her. Fate had played her a cruel trick, giving her back the right to love him, only to have him snatch it away again.

"But I do love him," she whispered into the darkness. "And he cannot be blamed when he is innocent of any wrongdoing." Her words were issued out into the room lit only by the faint moonlight, and as if they were a cork in a bottle, they released a flow of ideas.

Two heads were better than one, and two pairs of eyes could better observe Tully. Her major difficulty was trying to persuade herself that Tully was in truth the guilty party, but that would quite possibly be caused by her fondness for him, she knew. As Ondridge had said, who else could it be? Certainly, no one else stood to gain.

Meanwhile, even as one part of her mind explored the possibilities of Tully's guilt, the rest began to seethe in indignation that Ondridge should be so unjustly accused. Even if he never knew of her love, she was persuaded she must help to clear him of such unjust suspicion. Once her decision was made, she drifted into a peaceful sleep, undisturbed by dreams.

To the wonder of everyone gathered around the breakfast table the next morning, Rolissa entered looking none the worse for her previous night's experience. Lord Jamison, a large, portly gentleman with a shy, self-effacing manner, bowed solemnly to her and left the expressions of concern to his wife, who sat at the other end of the table. Most of the elderly guests either had elected to have their breakfasts in their rooms or had not yet risen. The table, liberally decked with spring flowers, was ringed by the younger members of the party who were gathered in preparation for a day's outing at the local abbey, famous for both its antiquity and its architecture.

Rolissa greeted Lord Plythford, who sat across from her, and Miss Singer, who looked a perfect picture in her blue muslin, with matching ribbons in her hair. Farther down the table, Jane Singer was engaged in a one-sided conversation with Tully, who was standing by her chair.

"Well, here is our runaway," Jamie said, as he entered the room through the French windows and held her chair for her.

"None the worse, Cousin?" Tully asked. He had turned from Jane to the buffet where he poured a cup of chocolate and carried it over to Rolissa, forestalling a footman who would have undertaken the service.

Rolissa shook her head, not quite trusting herself to speak to the man she had hitherto considered a friend. As she glanced up, she was taken by the worry lines on his face. His eyes appeared strained, and it occurred to her to wonder if the emotional wear had been apparent for some time, or if her notice of it was due to her heightened awareness.

"My dear, are you sure you should have left your bed?" asked Lady Jamison, who was not at all persuaded that Rolissa had not suffered more from her adventure than she was allowing to show.

Rolissa returned a warm smile, touched by her hostess's concern, but she was determined that she would not be made an invalid.

"Quite certain, and I am quite looking forward to the visit to the abbey."

"I, for one, am awed by your resilience." Jamie, who had taken the chair on the other side of Rolissa, spoke with more than a tinge of pomposity in his manner, his usual prelude to throwing a shaft at his bosom friend. "I will endeavour to dedicate myself to your entertainment. If I can keep my boon companion from boring you to tears, I trust we will have a pleasant outing." He stirred his coffee, glancing across the table at Tully, who was absently moving a kipper about on his plate.

"That is, if I can keep old Tully there from boring you to death, I think we will have a pleasant day," Jamie repeated, waiting for the return sally, which was not forthcoming.

Miss Singer, too, noticed the lack of response and turned anxious eyes on the viscount. "Sir, will you be accompanying us to the abbey?"

"I'm not sure." Tully suddenly pushed back his chair and rose abruptly. Making his excuses, he hurriedly left the room.

Plythford looked up from his plate, as if wondering what he had done to put Tully in a rage, since he himself was usually the guilty party. Jane Singer gazed at her sister with open curiosity, while that young woman, looking hurt and mortified, lowered her head and pretended to concentrate on her breakfast. Rolissa, carrying enough wounds on her own heart so that she could readily sympathise with another's troubles, felt a pang at the younger lady's discomfort. She tried to ease the situation.

"I fear I have ruined the party," she said remorsefully. "It was stupid of me to think I could control the coach and team, and all I succeeded in doing was to make additional difficulties. Now our charming escorts are fatigued from spending half the night searching for me."

The gratitude in Jamie's eyes showed he mistook her attempt to ease Miss Singer's hurt for an effort at covering Tully's sudden exit.

"That is part of it," he said jovially, "and it will be your responsibility to keep the party charming enough to prevent us from dozing, but I think Tully probably took a fall from his horse in the dark—not that he would tell *me* of it." With a laugh that sounded a bit forced, he excused himself and left the room just as Ondridge entered.

Lady Jamison gave the tardy breakfaster a beaming smile. "Our knight errant." She beamed. "We owe you a debt of gratitude, but I need to call upon you once more. I am convinced that Lady Rolissa should not attempt the journey to the abbey after her terrible experience."

"My dear lady, it is I that should have your cosseting," he replied as he bowed over her hand and moved off to inspect the buffet. "I am of the opinion that she took no lasting harm, but her fierceness when she took me for a highwayman left me in terror."

Rolissa kept her head bent over her breakfast, not knowing what invention Ondridge was adding to the previous night's adventure, but it was in her mind to let him handle it. Then, from the corner of her eye, she saw his gaze, and correctly guessed that he had backed himself into a corner. Delving into her own imagination for something to add, she toyed with a half-eaten piece of toast.

"How not?" she asked calmly. "It is excessively frightening to be walking on a dark track with trees blowing and suddenly a horseman approaches you out of the shadows."

"Oh, Lady Rolissa, you must be the bravest thing," Jane Singer cried out. "I declare, I would have been thrown into the vapours."

"Oh, but that was impossible," Rolissa answered. "I had used my entire supply long before. As of this morning, I am convinced that we each only have a limited capacity for terror at one time."

"Well, you could have had my share for the asking." Ondridge grinned. "The last thing I expected was to be threatened by a lady in a poke bonnet, brandishing a fallen limb from which she had stripped the branches. Most startling when you are half-asleep in the saddle."

His droll look brought smiles and laughs from the others, and Rolissa joined in. It only needed such a silly fabrication to lend authenticity to the explanation that had been given her foolish panic. And he was playing his part very well, she thought, though it could have been better done. The way his eyes kept meeting hers across the table, someone was certain to start talk about a *tendre* between them again, and the lightness of his attitude seemed to indicate some great weight had been lifted off his shoulders.

"Well, I hope to be forever spared such an experience." Miss Singer shuddered, and Rolissa could imagine the effort it took for her to join the conversation. "I am looking forward to exploring the countryside, but I prefer a gentle ride and a safe escort. I am not at all adventurous, I fear."

"I think you'll find it an interesting area," Ondridge said, "but I caution you, and everyone else—" he sobered as he gave a significant glance around the table—"to stay away from the ruins to the west. By the end of summer, we'll have them down, but they are highly dangerous at the moment. For your own safety, stay away from them."

Rolissa remembered passing them when she was on the coach, and shivered. The standing portions of the old stone walls, reaching into the evening sky like jagged fingers, were not what she considered the most pleasant sights in the area.

Young Jane Singer was more interested in the day's outing. "Are you joining on our trip to the abbey?" she asked Ondridge.

"I think I shall, now that I have overcome my fright of Lady Rolissa," he answered with a smile. "I was not sure this morning that I would not be thrown into a shaking at breakfast by the sight of her picking up a fork, she was so terrifying last night. But I see that I have ample room to dodge."

"I declare, my reputation will be quite ruined," Rolissa announced with mock asperity. "May I please go, if I allow myself to be forcibly restrained from doing damage to my knight errant?"

= 11 =

THE VISIT TO the abbey was not accounted a success. The abstraction that afflicted Rolissa, Tully, and Jamie, together with the solemn splendour of the ancient edifice, lowered the spirits of the entire party.

Miss Singer, shy or nervous at best, was convinced she had aroused the viscount's distaste for her and appeared to be constantly on the verge of tears. The younger Miss Singer, all her adoration for Lord Tulane evaporating in the face of her sister's misery, was hard-pressed to be civil to him, and eyed the rest of the party with misgivings. Rolissa longed to assure the brokenhearted young woman that Tully's distraction was not due to her, but since nothing other than the terrible truth would suffice to justify this sudden change of attitude in him, she considered the situation hopeless. Only she knew what pain the young lady would suffer if she were in possession of the truth.

Even Jamie was severely out of sorts. Several times, his attitude toward Rolissa seemed to verge on anger and contempt, but when it surfaced, it disappeared so quickly she could never be certain it had been there.

Plythford spent most of the following days in the saddle, riding about the countryside, and when he was in the company of the others at luncheon, dinner, and in the evenings, he appeared to be watching, listening for any hint of what had turned the earlier gaiety into tension and discomfort. Another watcher was Ondridge. He and Plythford made the principal effort to raise the spirits of the group, but without success.

The only truly interesting happening during this time was the sudden decision of Lord Amberly to purchase a carriage and hire a personal groom. When he followed this, for him, shocking extravagance with the acquisition of two new coats and a hat, Lady Jennie spent one evening regaling the party with conjectures on his coming profligacy. But even that very humourous speculation could not last for more than one evening, and the doldrums descended again.

On the fourth evening, when Rolissa was preparing to dress for dinner, Lady Jennie bustled into her room. The plump lady was a startling picture in bright yellow with green panniers, a style long out of fashion, but one that was expressly chosen by this paragon of eccentricity to wear in the country. The yellow turban that was clipped with a large ruby brooch slipped a bit as she shook her head in disgust.

"Just look at yourself, girl. Pretty as a picture, but the effect is ruined by that downcast look on your face. I can't think what's wrong with you young people. Time for us to move on to Brighton. We leave in the morning."

"Oh, Aunt Jennie, I don't think I want to." Rolissa walked to the window and stood looking out, not wanting to meet her aunt's eyes. She was unable to give an explanation without revealing the secret she had given Ondridge her word she would keep.

While she was standing, looking down into the garden, wondering what to say that would placate Lady Jennie, she saw Ondridge walk across the garden and slip through the hedge. In due course he met Soames, who came out the rear of the stables leading the earl's horse. She knew by the stealth that he was off to assure himself of the safety of the children.

While she was watching, there came a scratching on the door of Rolissa's room. Lady Jennie opened it to admit Lord Amberly.

"Has the decision to leave been agreed to?" he asked slyly, looking around as if he expected someone suddenly to appear and accuse them of conspiracy.

Lady Jennie threw up her hands, indicating her exasperation. "Rolissa wants to stay, though why, when there's such an epidemic of doldrums hung over the place, is beyond me."

"Really?" Lord Amberly looked surprised. "I was sure you would want to go, my dear. Certainly you would have a gayer time in Brighton, but whatever you ladies decide will do for me. There is a surprisingly adequate library here—" During this speech, he had been crossing the room, and now he stood close to Rolissa, peering at her face as if something he saw there concerned him.

"Jennie," he said hesitantly, "why do you not finish your preparations for dinner, and let me have a talk with Rolissa. My dear, you do look pulled."

The last thing Rolissa desired at the moment was a comforting chat with her elderly male cousin, but since he had never been one to try to sway her with his opinions, and his concern was evident, she knew no way of ridding herself of his company, short of giving him an undeserved snub. Since she could not alleviate his anxieties on her behalf, she cast an imploring glance at her aunt, hoping she would take him away with her, but for once Lady Jennie seemed at a loss.

"Well," the outspoken dowager vacillated, "don't harangue her, Henry. No point in making her more droopy in spirits than she is."

When Lady Jennie closed the door after leaving the room, Rolissa looked up into the myopic eyes of her cousin, wondering how she could turn the conversation and send him happily back to his researches. Since staring into his eyes for an indefinite period would be rude, she glanced out of the window, and was just in time to see Tully slipping through the garden hedge, heading for the second and older stable that was just beyond the one where Ondridge kept his horse. By the stealth of the viscount's movements, he, too, was slipping away, and the only reason to enter her mind was that he was following Ondridge.

"He couldn't know!" she cried out, and tried to pull away from Lord Amberly, but, perceiving her distress, he tightened his grip on her hands.

"Child, what causes you this suffering?" he asked, all concern.

"Henry, don't ask me," she implored. "I must go! I cannot explain, but a man's life may depend upon my speed." She tried again to free her hands, but he gripped all the tighter.

"A man's life!" He looked shocked and disbelieving. "What is it, is the stable on fire?" He peered through the small panes of the glass. "Shall I ring for the servants?"

"No, Henry, turn me loose, I must go!"

"I don't understand, but I am not letting you run into any danger. You have had one fright this visit, and I will not allow you another if I can prevent it."

Seeing no other way she could free herself, and trusting Henry to keep the secret with which Ondridge had entrusted her, she told him the complete story. ". . . and if you don't let me go, Tully may *kill* Ondridge," she said, as she struggled to free her hands.

"Such villainy!" Henry gasped, still keeping his grip. "But you cannot go—yes, you must, but not alone—what must we do—but, of course, I have a carriage now, don't I?" He threw back his shoulders and, as if making a sudden decision, he pulled her suddenly toward the door, as anxious as she to be on the way. In the passage, he paused only long enough to accost a footman, who ran to the stables carrying the urgent message that Lord Amberly's carriage should be made ready at once.

"Speak to no one, let me make our excuses," Henry instructed her as they hurried down the stair. "We must not start a scandal, you know. They are both family, or at least close connexions."

They were near the side door, and since the hour was such that it was unlikely visitors would call, there was only one footman on duty, and the guests were all in their quarters, preparing for dinner. It did not behoove Lord Amberly to make his excuses to a servant, so they rushed out into the garden and around the house just in time to see the lord's carriage led out. Lord Amberly handed Rolissa into the vehicle.

"To the ruins, Sammy," my lord directed his driver. "And make haste."

Rolissa was breathless from their run through the house, down the stairs, and out into the garden, so between the exertions and the worry that was flogging her, she did not mentally absorb the misdirection when it was first mentioned. They were down the avenue and across the public road, rolling along the twisted country tracks, when she realised what Lord Amberly had said.

"No, this is wrong, this isn't the direction," she cried out, as the carriage turned toward the ruins. "We should have taken the last turn to the left."

Lord Amberly leaned forward, his face showing extreme alarm. "Are you sure of your direction, Sammy?" he called to his driver.

"That I am, Gov'nor. When he rides out late like this, he comes in this direction. I seen him before."

"You've been having him watched?" Rolissa asked, wondering why Lord Amberly would so involve himself, but she was assured that

Sammy's occasional sights of Ondridge came from no more than his being a local who often used the roads himself, and since it seemed logical, Rolissa thought no more about it. Only minutes later, the wild ride came to a halt as they drew up near the jagged ruin of what looked, upon closer inspection, to be an old monastery.

Lord Amberly started to step down from the carriage and then hesitated, looking back at Rolissa.

"My dear, I hesitate to have you near so dangerous a spot, yet I cannot leave you alone here while Sammy and I go to the earl's aid—"

"You won't," Rolissa said with decision as she prepared to follow him from the carriage. "I am coming with you. I promise to be careful."

With a doubtful look in her direction, Lord Amberly climbed down and wove his way through the debris and brambles, heading for the walls. Rolissa followed in his footsteps, and after securing the reins to a tree, Sammy the groom brought up the rear of the procession. After slipping on several stones covered with lichen, and impatiently freeing her skirts from the briars of blackberry bushes, Rolissa trailed Lord Amberly as they bent to step beneath fallen timbers, until they were in a roofless area that had once been the sanctuary of a chapel. Lord Amberly turned, a pacific smile on his face, and nodded as he looked behind her. She turned to view the recipient of his silent message and saw Sammy, pointing a pistol directly at her.

"You see, Sammy"—Lord Amberly smiled at his groom—"it was much easier to let her come in by herself. It saved us the exertion of a struggle."

"I—I don't understand," Rolissa said haltingly. The truth was glimmering in the recesses of her mind, but it was at that moment blocked by the paralysing effect of her shock.

"It's very simple, my dear. The time has come for the Fortesques to come back into their own. The Amberlys have for too many generations held all the wealth in the family. For years I have read about their excesses, their haughty airs, how they have lorded it over my side of the family, giving a bit here and a bit there, salving their consciences, when historically we have been the poor relations. The time has come to change history."

"But it *has* changed," Rolissa said. "You now have the title and all the entailed properties—my father!" Suddenly, she saw that his fall from the horse had not been the unfortunate accident they had thought it. "Anson and Whippy!" In spite of her fear, she took a step toward him, but was forced back by the gun in Sammy's hand.

"Yes, your dear father," Lord Amberly said with a sigh. "You know, I did like James, and I'm rather sorry it had to be he, but the time had come to reverse the fortunes, you see—"

"Let's get on with it, Gov'nor," Sammy interrupted.

One look at Sammy's implacable face, and Rolissa knew she had to keep Lord Amberly talking, else a sudden period would be put to her life. Surely her elderly cousin was deranged; how else could he have committed so many and such horrible crimes and seem to bear no remorse? Had she read somewhere that you flattered and calmed an insane person? Her mind was in a muddle of fear and grief, but she forced out a question between trembling lips.

"But how could you do it?" she asked. "Certainly it was not easy to kill people and not leave some trail."

"Who notices servants?" Lord Amberly asked complacently. "Not even you noticed Sammy from the short time he worked at Amberly as an undergroom. A clever man is Sammy, and a dedicated man. Like me, he is tired of being overlooked because he is only someone to whom the wealthy Amberlys and the Lettons toss crumbs."

"And the Talmadges?" Rolissa asked, thinking of Anson.

"Talmadges?" Lord Amberly's brow wrinkled in a frown. "Pray absolve me—as far as I am aware, Anson did truly fall from his horse. Quite a surprise that. Understood he was a good rider. More than likely it was truly an accident."

"But why Whippy and now me?" Rolissa asked, still trying to buy time.

"You, I am very sorry about," Lord Amberly said, with every evidence of sadness. "I really had changed my plan, you know. It seems such a pity to destroy such loveliness, and I had decided that by getting your father's share from Whippy I would do just as well. I didn't know about the brats, worse luck, and then even if I managed to do away with them, the money was still left to you. So there is nothing for it but for you to have an accident."

"No one will believe it," Rolissa said, with more confidence than she felt.

"Oh, I think so, my dear. You see, while you were out on your famous adventure, you came by this ruin and discovered, just as it was growing dark, what you thought to be carved lintel. You brought me back here, believing it to be something useful to me in my research, and in our efforts to find it again, you ran up against one of these unstable beams. I will be desolated, of course. Amberly will, for some time, be a shrine to you and your father—the countryside will be touched that I cannot set foot in the place that so reminds me of my deceased loved ones, but it was, after all, just another accident."

Unnoticed by either Rolissa, Lord Amberly, or his groom, there were three interested witnesses to the abrupt departure of Lord Amberly's carriage, and three pairs of ears overheard the direction.

Only a few minutes later, a pounding of hooves through a small but dense wood lost its rhythmic beat and degenerated into a confusion of whinnying. Two horses nearly collided as Ondridge rode out from behind a cluster of bushes and intercepted his tiger, nearly causing the smaller man to lose his seat in surprise.

"Lord love you, Captain, you gave me a start, you did." Soames announced, trying to quiet his frightened horse.

"I ought to do more than that." Ondridge glowered at his groom. "What the devil do you mean, following me?"

Soames eyed his employer warily, wondering how he could admit what he knew and still turn the expected wrath from himself. He was not so devoted to the earl as to be blind to the fact that Ondridge could be a hard man if he thought his privacy was threatened or his plans thwarted without very good reason.

"It's like this, Captain. I'm thinking there may be a chance someone has tumbled to your lay." He gave Ondridge a quick explanation of Rolissa's and Lord Amberly's departure, and the directions he had overhead. ". . . I know that's not where you have them little gentry coves stashed, but it seems to me it's got something to do with them maybe—or—something—" He ducked his head as he mumbled the last few words. Facing the earl's direct gaze, he was unsure exactly what he had in mind, though he had been when he left Ivycroft. "Anyway, it seemed to me that something was havey-cavey, and you should know," he ended lamely.

"Doesn't make sense." Ondridge shook his head, but his attention immediately returned to his tiger. He scowled. "And how did you know about the Letton twins, or that I had them stash— hidden?" he demanded.

"Well, shut me down, Captain, ain't it my duty to know where you are, seeing how's it's a tiger's duty to be on hand—" He flinched as Ondridge raised his hand with the riding crop, but the gesture was to stop his explanation. The earl's eyes were thoughtful.

"Their sudden dash wouldn't have anything to do with the children," Ondridge surmised. "I can't believe she would tell Amberly about them, and if she did, they wouldn't be heading for the ruins—good God! Have I been a blind fool!" He jerked his horse around so suddenly that the animal reared in surprise.

"Soames, are you armed?"

"Aye, that I am, Captain, and right behind you if there's trouble coming."

Soames was forced to shout his last words over the receding hoofbeats of the earl's mount. As much by the power of his own will as the ability of the animal he rode, the tiger was able to keep close behind Ondridge as he turned his course and headed for the ruins, but they were separated by the first fence they encountered. While the blooded hunter ridden by Ondridge sailed over the obstruction, the hack Soames rode balked, and the tiger was too accomplished a rider and a judge of horseflesh to put the animal at an obstacle it could not overcome. Knowing he would have to find his own way, he turned aside, cursing the mount under him as he looked for a gate.

Tommy, or Thomas Renville Anderson Smithington, Earl of Plythford, was waiting out a week at Ivycroft for reasons best known to himself and the only two people in his confidence. He was restless, anxious to be on his way, and since the house party had digressed into something closely resembling a wake, he sought refuge in riding about the countryside as much as possible. Several times, he had considered cutting his visit short, but a wit far less sharp than his would have noticed there was something amiss, and it concerned several people for whom he had a liking.

Rolissa, as he had described her to Jamie in a moment of levity, was walking around as if she had lost her last fortune. Jamie had, for courtesy's sake, tried to smile at the sally, but he, too, was under a cloud of worry. Being a man who was normally observant and interested in his friends, Plythford had seen the looks Jamie threw in the visount's direction, and had correctly surmised Tully to be the major reason for Jamie's concern. Slightly more attention to the group told him Rolissa, too, was watching Tully, and Ondridge was keeping a close eye on all of them. Altogether, their unusual behaviour sometimes made the house party as interesting as it was morose.

It could not be considered wonderful, then, that on returning from a ride in time to dress for dinner, and just having paused at the eaves of the wood, Plythford was intrigued to see Ondridge ride out from behind the stables, staying close to a high hedge that shielded him from any eyes that might be looking from the house. Plythford's mild curiosity was piqued considerably when Tully, similarly furtive, appeared and rode along in Ondridge's wake.

For a moment, he considered intercepting Ondridge to let him know he had a follower, and then thought better of it. He had never believed the rumours, but it could not be thought wonderful if Tully did and was out after proof that Ondridge had killed his brother. Plythford grinned as he thought that the viscount would be more likely to walk in on Ondridge and one of his inamoratas. He shook his head in regret as he started for the stables. If he was right in his surmise, the confrontation should be something to see.

He was just coming up by the stables, approaching from the rear, when he saw Rolissa and Lord Amberly driving off and heard the direction called to the driver. That Rolissa was frightened of something was apparent, even from that distance, but that something did not appear to be Lord Amberly. Still, Plythford could not like it that they were heading for a place Ondridge had warned all the party against, saying it was unsafe. He swung his mount to the opposite side of the hedge and followed.

Ondridge was capable of taking care of himself, Plythford thought, but Rolissa had no business at those ruins. Some vague suspicion lurked in his mind, more a sense of unfitness than any idea of concrete danger, but he decided to hang back, to cut through the wood and keep enough distance between himself and the carriage so he could oversee their movements while he himself remained unobserved.

The third person to see the carriage leave and overhear the direction was Jamie. He had been walking in the garden, ready to enter the house after seeing Tully on his way as he followed Ondridge. The morning after Rolissa's adventure, he had browbeaten the distraught Tully until he found out what was bothering his friend, and had become an ally. Knowing that Ondridge and Rolissa suspected his boon companion of guilt in the murders had made it nearly impossible for him to be pleasant to them, yet he could see where they might feel justified. His peace had been sorely cut up.

He, too, was alarmed that the announced destination was a place they had been warned not to go, and a suspicion of most definite porportions entered his mind. He raced for the stable, but as luck would have it, there was not even a stable boy in sight, since it was their dinner hour.

By the time he had saddled his own horse, which was faster than finding someone to do it for him, and had galloped down to the junction of the avenue and the public road, the carriage was no longer in sight. He looked around, frowning and wondering where to head next.

Though his family had leased Ivycroft for three years during the summer, he usually spent the warmer months in Cornwall on an estate his grandmother had left him, so he was not at all familiar with the countryside. His only chance of reaching the ruins without calling out one of the servants to direct him was to locate Tully, who had given him a reasonably good idea of the path he would take in following Ondridge. Luckily, it would take him in the same general direction.

A breathless ride in which he crammed his fences and endangered himself and his mount brought him soon into sight of Tully, who glowered at him.

"Cawker," the viscount snapped. "What if you'd run into Ondridge? He'd be sure you were in it with me to smother the brats."

"Forget both Ondridge and the brats," Jamie gasped, not taking time to catch his breath before launching into his explanation. "The one thing we forgot in all this was that Rolissa's father was the first to be killed." He told Tully what had happened.

"Good Lord!" Tully immediately wheeled his horse, leaving Jamie to follow.

Jamie raced after the viscount, as anxious as he to reach the ruins before some harm could come to Rolissa. They were just coming to the edge of the wood, and through the trees the brighter light signified open land and faster travel when Tully checked his pace. Ahead was a ravine too wide to jump, and at that particular place the sides were too steep to negotiate.

"Just what we needed," Tully growled. "We'll have to follow it until we find a crossing."

But they had ventured only a few paces when Tully, who was still leading, pulled his pistol from his belt and fired at something ahead. Jamie, looking up, saw only the rump of a horse as it disappeared into a thicket. Both he and Tully dismounted, and since he was unarmed, Jamie grabbed the reins of the viscount's horse while Tully reloaded. They both ducked as they heard the sound of a shot, and a bullet whizzed close by. While Tully kept watching in the direction in which he had fired, Jamie gave a cautious look around, thinking the shot aimed at them had come from the other direction.

"Who is it?" Jamie asked, creeping closer to his friend.

"Who do you think? I knew that fellow was up to no good. No reason for him to be here, no reason at all."

Jamie was ready to let Tully know his answer had hardly been enlightening, but a movement in the thicket caused Tully to fire again before he could say as much.

The answering shot was immediate, and as Jamie had suspected, it came from the opposite direction. This time there was no doubt, since it went through the fleshy part of Jamie's left arm and buried itself in the bark of the tree in front of him.

He cried out in pain and anger, dropping the reins, whereupon the frightened horses bolted. Tully gaped at the fleeing horses and the blood welling out of the hole in his friend's coat.

"Why shoot Jamie? He's not even armed!" Tully roared as if he had been personally insulted.

Jamie, busy holding his arm, glared at his companion, thinking that if anyone had the right to be outraged, it was he, since he had been wounded. But his irritation was overcome by surprise as they received an immediate answer.

"Sorry, Gov'nor, didn't know it was you," came a call that Jamie recognized as Soames's. "But I'll tell you, my lord, you keep shooting at the captain, and I'll have *you* in me sights quick enough."

"Ondridge?" Tully ejaculated. "I was shooting at Plythford!"

"And *I'd* damn well like to know why!" came a call from the other direction. "I'm not armed, either!"

By this time, Soames had come out of hiding and was leading his mount. "It ain't the captain over there?" he asked suspiciously, and then glared at Tully. "Cork-brained to go popping off at Lord Plythford."

"You impudent devil, you're a fine one to talk after shooting Jamie," retorted Tully, dividing his attention among Jamie, Soames, and Plythford, who was hurrying up and pulling off his neckcloth to use as a bandage on Jamie's arm. Satisfied that Plythford could look after Jamie, he turned to Soames. "I need that animal," he said, trying to take the reins away from the tiger.

"Well, you ain't getting it," Soames replied. "I'm on the captain's business. Like as not, both he and his gentry mort'll be done for while I'm messing around with you." Soames backed away and climbed into the saddle, but Tully was too quick for him. When the tiger turned the horse, Tully grabbed the croup and pulled himself up behind the saddle.

"Then I'm going with you," Lord Tulane said. "You need my weapon."

"I wouldn't be thinking anybody that pops off like you is needed anywhere, my lord," Soames grumbled as he urged the horse forward.

Plythford, who had made a sketchy but adequate job of bandaging Jamie's arm, helped the wounded man mount behind his saddle.

"Not that we'll do any good, but we might as well tag along," he said, putting the horse to a trot.

"Neither of us armed and me shot," Jamie said with disgust, "but keep up. If nothing else, we can referee those two."

"Just another accident," Lord Amberly had said.

"Just another accident?" At first Rolissa had thought she heard an echo, but how could an echo carry the uplifted tones of question, and how could it be in Ondridge's voice? She thought she had been deceived by the combination of fear and hope, but if she had, then it had also fooled her captors, because Lord Amberly swore softly, and Sammy turned toward the shadowy doorways at the rear of the chapel. He raised his pistol, looking for a target, but there was no one visible.

"Stay back!" Rolissa cried, her heart pounding with hope, but afraid Ondridge would meet the same fate they had planned for her. "He's armed and—"

Her shout drew the groom's attention back to her, and she blanched as he swung the barrel in her direction. But before he had taken aim, there came a report and a flash from the dimness, and Sammy dropped his weapon, cursing as the blood welled up through his jacket. After one final look in the direction from which the shot originated, he turned and began to run toward the entrance. Even before Sammy had turned to flee, Lord Amberly was scrambling over the loose and fallen stones. Neither had covered more than half the distance, but Sammy had come abreast of the fleeing man when Lord Amberly ran forcefully into a half-fallen timber.

Then Rolissa saw Ondridge as he appeared from the dark passage and came rushing toward her. Thankfully, she raised her arms, but her feet seemed to be suddenly too heavy to move; there was a roaring in her ears. Ondridge was shouting as he ran, pointing toward the sky, so she looked to see the wildly swaying wall as it undulated like a grain field in the wind. Then she, too, swayed, and was lost in the peacefulness of oblivion.

She awoke to the secure feeling of someone holding her in his arms, and as she opened her eyes the first thing she beheld was Ondridge looking down at her, one hand stroking her hair. The eyes that gazed into hers held such tenderness and concern that, not caring if she might be forward, she reached up. Using one forefinger, she tried to smooth away the creases of worry on his brow.

There was so much she wanted to say, but as the last line in his face seemed to disappear under the movement of her hand, only two words passed her lips.

"It's over."

"Yes, my darling, it's over." He seemed about to say more, but at the thudding of hoofbeats he looked up. She turned her head to see Soames and Tully as they rounded the side of the ruins and came to a stop where Ondridge sat on the grass with Rolissa in his arms.

"Knew you could do it, Captain," Soames announced as he dismounted. "I'd of been here sooner but for his lordship here."

A second horse, carrying Plythford and Jamie, rounded the corner of the ruin. Plythford brought the animal to a plunging halt and both gentlemen dismounted.

"Are you two all right?" Plythford asked.

"In perfect health, thank you," Ondridge replied, eyeing the new arrivals. "Is this some new fashion? Why all this companionship on horseback?"

"Wouldn't have had to, if a certain lord I know didn't go around shooting at people." Soames gave Tully a dark look.

"No, we wouldn't, and we wouldn't have lost the other two horses if you hadn't shot Jamie!"

Ondridge gazed at his tiger with astonishment. "Now why the devil would you shoot Jamie?"

"You just asked me if I had a barker," Soames muttered into his chest. "You didn't say where I was to point it."

"And next time I would appreciate it if you would *tell* him," Jamie said, glowering down at Ondridge as if he had pulled the trigger. "But I'm still trying to decide what happened here. What happened to Amberly? He was the one behind it all, wasn't he?"

"He was," Ondridge said slowly. "But he was caught in his own trap. From what I gathered from his conversation, he intended to pull the wall down on Rolissa, probably rendering her unconscious first. But when I winged his groom, he panicked and ran into one of the timbers, dislodging it. They're both under there—somewhere."

Jamie stared at the fallen wall and shook his head. "And no one suspected him at all until this evening." He looked from Ondridge to Tully. "You didn't, did you?"

Tully looked sheepish. "Some Bow Street Runners we'd make. I was after you all the time, and you were after me."

"You knew?" Ondridge looked up, frowning.

"Not until the night Rolissa was lost," Tully replied, smiling down at her. "I was searching for you when I found the house. I was just looking around, to see if you could have taken shelter there, and overheard your talk. That was what completely overset me." He gazed at Ondridge. "If you had the Letton boys, then you couldn't have done in Whippy, and if not Whippy, then not Anson. Of course, I couldn't blame you for your suspicions of me. But then I've been in a real taking over who it *could* have been."

"What I don't understand is what you thought *I* had to do with it," Plythford complained to Tully. "Or did you just fire on me out of general principles?"

"Didn't connect you with it at all until I saw you in the woods," Tully said. "Then I figured you were in on it, because I never have understood why you were down here."

"If I thought you could keep your mouth closed I'd *tell* you, provided it would keep you from shooting at me for another three days," Plythford growled.

"He'll keep quiet," Ondridge said, grinning at the sparks in the eyes of Plythford and Tully. "He'll be so glad to know you're not trying to run off with Rolissa, he'll be delighted." He grinned up at the others and then down at Rolissa. "As a matter of fact, he's up to his old tricks, trying to run off with an heiress again."

Jamie shook his head. "Not another one, Tommy."

"Same one," Plythford said, kicking a clump of dirt with one well-polished boot toe as the society pose momentarily disappeared in a small-boy shyness.

Ondridge laughed. "You have to give Plythford credit. He keeps trying. The first time he stole her from the schoolroom, but he was just reading for Oxford himself. The second time he was still in his salad days when her father had betrothed her to someone else. Maybe now he's old enough to manage it, especially since a widow is not as closely guarded as a debutante. You realise all this has been with her permission, of course."

Rolissa had been letting the conversation flow over her head, too glad to be alive and braced in the crook of Ondridge's arm to care about anything else, but one word had brought her back to reality.

"A widow?" She looked up in surprise.

Ondridge, who suddenly could not seem to keep a smile off his face, nodded. "Lady Handing. They've been in love for years. She was a good wife to a close friend of mine, but I always thought her heart was somewhere else. Several weeks ago she confided in me, and I have been running a rig to keep the attention off Tommy. I purchased a special license before leaving London so Tommy wouldn't be suspected. A few days from now, he'll meet her in Norwich, where she'll be shopping, and they'll be off and married before anyone can stop them this time—we hope." He gave the blushing Plythford a doubtful look that brought a chuckle from Jamie.

"Lord, I don't believe it!" Tully looked stunned at the revelation.

"You would if you could see past your nose," Jamie retorted. "Lot you can say anyway, since you'll be trying to beat Ondridge and Rolissa to the altar, now that you've offered for Miss Singer."

"Damn it, Jamie!" Ondridge ejaculated. "Take the others and go see to the horses."

"But we got the cattle right here, Captain," Soames pointed out.

"Now who's a cork-brain?" Tully demanded with unnecessary force. "Come on, you rodent."

As the others walked away, Rolissa raised her eyes to Ondridge. "But I thought *you* and she—" Rolissa let the words trail off. Even if he wasn't going to marry the widow, there was still the statement he had made the night she discovered the twins. All through the explanations his arms had been around her shoulders, but she shifted, pulling free. Even though she kept her eyes on her skirt, she could feel his attention.

She tried to stand, but Ondridge pulled her back to sit beside him. He put his arm around her again, and using his other hand, he raised her chin so their gazes met.

"I spent a great deal of time with Lady Handing to throw dust in the eyes of her relatives," he said. "And I was so angry at you. I was afraid Plythford would decide he wanted you instead. I couldn't understand how he could be around you, where I wanted to be, and not fall in love with you."

"I thought you were in love with her," Rolissa was repeating herself, hoping he would deny it again—such beautiful words.

"You should have known the truth. I tried to make you an offer before and you stopped me. Then, after Whippy's death, I thought I was next on the list, since I had not considered your father as one of the victims. I could not in good conscience endanger you, or any other woman."

"Oh, what a tangle," Rolissa replied, looking over at the fallen wall for the first time.

Ondridge turned her face away from the place where Lord Amberly had paid for the fear and deaths he caused.

"A tangle that is now unraveled," he said softly. "I would like to take two of the ends and tie up a neat little package, if you think you could see your way clear to accepting a man who will never make a Bow Street Runner, and who comes with a ready-made family of twin boys. And, of course, everyone will say, since I lost the Letton fortune, I married you for your inheritance, you know."

Rolissa, so filled with emotion, could only resort to that bubbling spirit within her, or dissolve in tears. She blinked the beginnings of moisture out of her eyes as she smiled at him.

"Talk about your fortune hunters." Her voice quivered with laughter and suppressed emotions. "Not only must your wife be wealthy, but even the children come hosed and shod."

His lips descended on hers for a long, delightful moment. When he again met her eyes, his were twinkling.

"That's called good management, my dear."

*If you have enjoyed this book and would like to
receive details of other Walker Regency romances,
please write to:*

Regency Editor
Walker and Company
720 Fifth Avenue
New York, N.Y. 10019